DEVIL'S MEADOW

Center Point Large Print

**This Large Print Book carries the
Seal of Approval of N.A.V.H.**

DEVIL'S MEADOW

Lauran Paine

CENTER POINT PUBLISHING
THORNDIKE, MAINE

This Center Point Large Print edition
is published in the year 2008 by arrangement with
Golden West Literary Agency.

The text of this Large Print edition is unabridged. In other
aspects, this book may vary from the original edition.
Printed in the United States of America.
Set in 16-point Times New Roman type.

ISBN: 978-1-60285-195-5

Library of Congress Cataloging-in-Publication Data

Paine, Lauran.
   Devil's meadow / Lauran Paine.--Center Point large print ed.
      p. cm.
   ISBN 978-1-60285-195-5 (lib. bdg. : alk. paper)
      1. Large type books. I. Title.

PS3566.A34D485 2008
813'.54--dc22

2008004211

CONTENTS

1
SURVIVAL

They passed across an acatillo plain, being selective of their route, then angled along the sidehill of a place that smelled of snakes, and where undoubtedly, because it was that time of year, rattlers were under the flat stones and amid the rocky jumbles shedding their skin, blind now and more deadly than at any other time.

Their horses were tucked up and caked with dry salt-sweat, head-hung in their exhaustion, aware of the snake-scent and too dulled from hard usage to care.

Dawn had arrived a half-hour earlier. The morning was blessedly cool, but on the south desert this time of year it was the only time of day which was cool.

They had been in the saddle since the morning before. So had the six-man posse on their back-trail. It had long since ceased to be a race; now it was simply a matter of pure endurance, a little luck, and whatever wiles Doria and Spencer possessed, with the odds about even—those were experienced possemen back yonder—and with the goal another thirty, forty miles ahead—the Mex line.

There was not another thirty or forty miles left in either horse. Ten, maybe, but no more than that.

Where they angled across a catclaw top-out Jim Doria looked back, then pointed.

There they were, still coming, all six of them in a

dogged walk riding their worn-down horses into the ground exactly as the outlaws were also doing. Paul Spencer said, "I never saw anything like it," and kept his horse moving across the rim and down the opposite slope. "Those bastards are never going to give up."

The light was poor. Visibility was actually down to about a mile but the sun was coming, was sending forth in advance lancing great trumpet-shaped flares of pink-gold brilliance.

Shortly now those possemen would cross over in the same spot Doria and Spencer had crossed the catclaw ridge, and with the sun at their back they would be able to discern the dusty, soiled pair of outlaws on ahead a few miles. Then the walking-race would begin all over again exactly as it had been going on for twenty-four hours now, and more.

It was open country. There was acatillo and occasionally a field of lacy paloverdes but there were no real trees except around the scarce settlements, man-planted and man-tended otherwise they would not be on the south desert, and then they could only live where water was handy, which was something else very precious and uncommon on the south desert.

The heat-haze never actually faded down here, between the seasons. It lay veil-like across all the devil's landscape softening the sharpness of scabrous mountains which stood far southward in Mexico. But at dawn the haze was not as pronounced as it was any other time of the day.

Towns existed, commonly distant from one another, and only where they had always existed, first as Indian villages around waterholes or running springs, then as Mexican settlements, and finally as the towns of the latest owners, the *Americanos*. But the towns could not expand beyond the ability of their water source to keep pace, which meant that except in very rare cases the towns and villages were not very much larger now than they had been two hundred years before.

In many places there were hundreds of miles between towns. In other places there were the ruins of ranches and villages which had been attacked and gutted so many times by the lords of the south desert, the Apaches, that they had never come back. Now, these ghost towns stood in ancient silence, their ruins untouched for fifty years, evidence of the terror and horror still lying here and there.

The Indians had been gone for many years now—except for bands of holdouts living south of the border who still raided northward now and then—but a population which was preponderantly Mexican would not rebuild those places of terror and tragedy because of the lamentations of the dying and the screams of the tortured, still to be heard on summer nights with a full moon, or so the Mexicans claimed anyway.

Doria had been through here twice before. Spencer never had, and when they paused at a cottonwood spring to tank up the horses, Spencer said if he lived to be a hundred he would not return to this country.

Then he rolled a smoke for breakfast with the last dust from his tobacco sack, flung the sack aside and lit up looking back. They were back there. This time he could not see them because of a low, bony ridge, but they were back there. It was one of the rare times over the past couple of days when he looked back, that he had not been able to either see them, or their dust.

"Gawddamndest bunch I ever heard of," he said, and wagged his head. "I'll lay odds they're going to follow us right down into Mexico." He coughed, spat, pitched away the cigarette and considered his horse. "Hey, Jim; I'm goin' to be afoot in another four, five miles."

Doria sank to one knee to sluice water over his face and head. The sun was reaching over each rim now, was making eerie little smoke-like shadows beyond the spidery paloverdes and around the flaking ancient big rocks.

Doria arose, looked back, saw nothing back there and crushed on his hat as he turned toward his resting horse. He grinned, dark eyes on his partner. "You reckon it's too late for us to put ourselves up for adoption to a rich widow?"

They pushed the horses beyond the grassy place heading as they always had headed, due southward, and they rode as though they fully expected to get down there, which was the only way for them to ride unless they decided to accept the alternative—captivity—and they had two good reasons for not wanting to even think about captivity. One reason was in the bulging saddlebags on Doria's horse. The other reason was a sprawled body in a dusty roadway many miles back, out front of the bank building in the town of Rosario.

They were two miles southeastwards of the last waterhole with some charred, roofless adobe ruins dead ahead when a flat, dull pulsation of sound reached down to them. Spencer drew rein in surprise, and twisted in the saddle. There was no sign of the six possemen but that had been the unmistakable sound of a gunshot.

Jim Doria tipped his hat to squint far back too, then said, "Rattlesnake. They wouldn't waste lead tryin' for us at this range. They came rode up onto a rattler."

It was reasonable. Paul urged his horse onward, riding loose and feeling distinctly uncomfortable because he liked animals and what they were doing to these two horses bothered him. He held out a hand for Doria's tobacco sack, and while rolling the smoke he said, "We'd ought to get out of this business, Jim."

Doria offered no argument. "Yeah. Times like these I think like that too. Only right now we can't get out of it. Not with that bunch behind us. Who the hell are they? I never in my life saw a posse stay on a trail like those fellers are doing. We've covered a hell of a lot of miles. Any other bunch of cowmen or townsmen would have called it quits long ago. Those bastards are hangin' on for dear life."

"Maybe they're Pinkerton detectives. This is how Pinkertons do it—just ride folks down even if they have to kill ten horses to do it."

11

"Naw. There weren't any Pinkertons in Rosario. Hell, the nearest Pinkerton agency is a thousand miles from Rosario."

"The army then," suggested Spencer and got a long look from Jim Doria.

"You ever see the army wearing suit coats and derby hats?"

Doria took back his tobacco sack and looped both reins to also build a cigarette. "If they're head-hunters, then they must have already been in Rosario when we raided the bank." He lit up. "And that'd be a hell of a coincidence."

Paul scratched, looked out and around, and said, "How much farther?"

Doria could only guess. "Thirty miles."

Spencer sighed. "We'll never make it. Never in gawd's green world." He continued to search the landscape. "Where's the nearest town?"

Jim Doria gestured indifferently. "On ahead."

"Yea. I figured it'd be on ahead. But *where*—on ahead?"

"Well, I'm not exactly sure. The last time I was down here I wasn't lookin' for a town. I think there's a Mex town a little more to the east, maybe six or eight more miles, though."

Paul Spencer trickled smoke, looked back, looked ahead, trickled more smoke and leaned to sympathetically stroke the neck of his horse. "I hate doin' this to my horse. We could set up an ambush and maybe scatter the bastards."

12

"And with odds like three-to-two—and with sacrificin' our lead—you know how that would end up?"

Paul did not reply. He smashed the cigarette atop his saddlehorn and pitched the thing away. "We better find that Mex town, then. Maybe we can buy some help down there. Don't they sell out pretty cheap here? I've heard that said. And we got the money."

"I wish this damned money was back in their bank and we were sittin' on a cutbank somewhere danglin' our naked feet in a creek of cold water."

Paul stood in his stirrups. "Trees!"

Doria looked hard, then aimed his tired horse in that direction. "Must be the Mex town," he said. "All right. We got no choice anyway. Maybe we can buy some fresh horses over there."

2
YELMO CAÑON

Calvo Sotelo knew the desert. His father had come here to escape the wrath of the Generalissimo years earlier. His father had not known at the time that he was no longer in Mexico. There were no boundary markers in those days.

Now there were—little piles of stones the U.S. Army Topographical Corps had stacked up and had whitewashed at far intervals. Even so, people came and went as they always had, either between the little white cairns or by ignoring them.

It had been a matter of indifference to the natives of

this immense barren south desert territory who owned the land for time out of mind, and even those who had owned it before hadn't pressed their claims. Except for thin stands of springtime grass, and an occasional mine, there was little to recommend the land to anyone. The *Norteamericanos* had changed much of that, true, but the basic essentials for existence remained unalterably indifferent and while the *gringos* had made more roads, had brought in freight, had herded cattle through during the grass-season, and had to some extent brought the south desert forward two hundred years, the amount of available water remained as it always had, the key to everything, and as Calvo Sotelo had often said during his hard years of existence down here, it still did not matter who owned the country, water alone was king.

He had goats, two burros, with wise-sad faces, and an adobe house of three rooms. Calvo was a man—among the Mexicans anyway—of substance even though he owned two pairs of pants, two shirt-blouses, and one pair of *huarachas,* and almost nothing else.

Years back the *Norteamericano* soldiers had hired him to scout for them during the Indian troubles. Once, he had been shot through the body in a skir-mish. Another time he had been cornered by two broncos in the canyon of the pumas, had emerged alive simply because the big blond soldier riding with him had got a horse shot dead under him, so they had to fight it out on foot, and the big blond soldier had become an enraged demon over the loss of that horse;

had shot it out almost toe to toe with the Apaches, and had afterwards beheaded them both.

Calvo knew ancient tales. He also had a number of his own to tell. When he told stories at all, which was not often. He was in his sixties now, still taller than most Mexicans and as sinewy as rawhide. As tough, they said, as *Señor Satán* himself.

No one knew the south desert any better than Calvo Sotelo. Occasionally, they still came to him for scouting, for manhunting, for hunting down lost and strayed cattle and horses, but Calvo no longer had much heart for some of the things which in his youth had meant so much to him. The south desert—the entire world for all Calvo knew—was not, after all, a place where it was essential for good to always triumph over evil. The world was instead, a place where people strove to survive, to remain healthy, to believe in their God even though He certainly was indifferent to most prayers, and along towards the end of it all, to chuckle because they had managed to make it into the sundown years, living with both good and evil, still with good vision, with strong teeth, with sound limbs and wind.

The devil was less a demon than he was a temptation. A man who had lived as long as Calvo had, upon innumerable occasions had met the devil face to face. A man never had to barter his soul, he simply had to realize that accommodation was essential to survival.

Well; the day he found the Spanish mine he had been trying to find a suitable place to conceal a horse he had stolen from a drunken Mexican *vaquero*. The Lord would never have rewarded a horsethief, but there was the mineshaft secreted behind a creosote thicket.

He later sold the horse to some *gringo* freighters who winked as they handed him over the silver dollars. Even *gringos* realized that a man in ragged britches and patched *huarachas* would never be able to own such a horse unless he had stolen it.

The devil was not always an enemy.

Since those days he had approached the old mineshaft from ten dozen different directions so there would never be a marked trail for someone to follow, and he had scratched with his broken knife and his bare hands at the seamy little gritty veins of dull gold.

It was a very old mine, clearly, and he called it the *yelmo* shaft because fifty feet back in the large, dark, cool tunnel he had found a broken Spanish casque, and the word in Spanish for a helmet was *yelmo*.

There was gold, he was sure of that, but he lacked the tools to deepen and lower the shaft. Not that it mattered. Calvo Sotelo was not a greedy man. He prised loose flakes and occasionally a respectable dull nugget. Mostly, he hoarded it; kept it hidden under the earthen floor of his shack in town, carefully stored in soiled little discarded tobacco sacks he had found along the roadways. The most certain way to get one's bare feet roasted over a little fire while one's arms were bound, was to allow a rumor to start that one had a cache of gold.

But someday he would go to Mexico City and live for a while like a grand *patrón*. Someday.

Meanwhile he went out with one of his burros every week or so to gather faggots which he would sell by the burro-load around town for firewood—and inside the loose blouse he wore was hidden one of the soiled little discarded tobacco sacks, full of gold.

But not always. Some days he simply sat in the cool shaft and ate a meager noon-day meal, or smoked a little, looked out where the fierce sunlight was curling the world in dancing waves of heat, and considered the indifference of his burro to its poor choice of food in the *yelmo* canyon.

It was a Godforsaken place. He had oftened wondered how the old Spaniards had known to come precisely to this narrow, desolate, stony, inhospitable canyon to make their shaft and find their gold. They were learned men, otherwise they would never have gone beyond sitting their saddles upon the low, sterile rim to look down into this secret place.

The *Norteamericanos* had a saying: 'gold is where you find it'. It was true, but what Calvo Sotelo never ceased to marvel about was how people knew where it was.

He leaned in the wonderful freshness of a spring-time day, back to the wall of his tunnel, considering the cacti-slopes leading down into this ten or fifteen acre open area, imagining how those old Spaniards had looked, picking their way back and forth through the spiny undergrowth, *armas* protecting their legs and the chest of their horses from the sharp spines which seemed to grow out of every variety of growth on the south desert.

They had carried muskets—*escopetas*—of course, and the little heavy swords with brass handles Spaniards had seldom gone without.

They were bearded, some swarthy, some fair as many *gringos* were, and they wore their hair long and clubbed or plaited, sometimes even cut short, but not often.

They were sturdy, muscular men, predatory and rapacious, brave and cunning. Calvo knew stories from his father, who had in turn got the same stories from his father and grandfather. He sat there day-dreaming in the gloomy, cool old shaft with its immeasurable depth of silence. Just on the other side of this silence lived the ghosts of people, in this case those old-time *genté de razón,* those gentlemen of reason.

Calvo's cigarette died in his fingers, his burro raised its head and for a long while considered the north-westerly rim, and a ragged old carrion-eating *sopilote* glided across, banking with perfect grace so that he might be able to scan the entire little place before the rising air carried him elsewhere.

Shadows lengthened, the heat, which would not be bad for another month or two yet, because this was springtime on the south desert, did not go beyond a very pleasant and comfortable livability, and when Calvo suddenly opened his eyes, it was not Spaniards picking their way downslope it was two *gringos* on exhausted horses, strangers and soiled, unkempt ones at that.

He was motionless in his cool, dark place, dark eyes fixed upon the horsemen who had evidently seen his burro down in the canyon. He cursed about that. But it still did not have to mean much. Even if they stole his burro, it would be a cheap price to pay to retain his secret. But cowboys did not steal burros.

The riders reached his flat area and swung to the ground, loosened cinchas and let their horses drink at Calvo's tiny trickling-spring where it kept a concave rock full. They spoke a little but he could not make out the words. They were not old men as he had first thought, but they were unshaven and gaunt, worn men whose guns seemed very heavy.

One of them scooped the hollow rock empty and waited until it had refilled after the horses, then tossed down his hat and lay prone to drink. The second one waited, turning to slowly consider the hidden place. Then he too drank while the other one stood looking up and around.

Calvo pushed out his lips in a silent whistle. He knew this kind. They were forever passing southward in a hurry, like wraiths.

Then his burro decided he did not like the newcomers. He did not go closer out of customary burro-inquisitiveness to examine the strangers and their animals, he decided instead to seek his owner and went walking on his little hooves back and forth until he was behind the great flourishing creosote bush which completely hid the mouth of the mineshaft.

He poked his dolorous long furry face into the entrance and peered at Calvo. He did not enter because the place smelled stale and because he was not fond of dark tunnels.

Behind him a man said, "Where did that jackass go?" and a second voice answered. "Over yonder, behind that big bush."

Calvo scarcely breathed.

"He didn't act like a wild jackass," that first man said. His companion answered shortly. "He wasn't wild. Probably belongs to some Mex. They got a lot of them down here."

"He's sure takin' his time behind that bush."

"Maybe he thinks he's hiding from us."

"I'm going over there."

Calvo listened, making out a word now and then. He understood English as well as Spanish, but being inside his mineshaft inhibited sounds, even when they were being made by men who were close by.

It was the burro who gave Calvo a clue. The little animal stepped back and turned to gaze westward and Calvo heard the soft ring of spurs with small rowels. One moment later he saw the rawboned, wide shoulders hunch as the face appeared.

They looked steadily at one another, the *gringo* so surprised he did not seem to breathe for a moment. Then he said, "Hey, partner, what you doin' in there?"

The second one walked quickly; Calvo's fear was

solidly physical, not especially for himself but for his gold mine.

The second one had dark hair and eyes and a hide burned bronze from summer suns. He too peered inside and for a moment he seemed as astonished as his companion had been, then he spoke almost matter-of-factly.

"You live in that cave, mister?"

Calvo shook his head. "No. I live in the town south of here. It is cool here." He arose, drew himself to his full height and walked forth into the sunlight with the pair of rangeriders staring at him. He smiled at them. "The town of Soledad," he murmured and gestured vaguely southward.

One of them turned and stepped inside the shaft, raised an arm to brush the stone ceiling, then turned and quickly said, "We might make it after all, Paul. It's big enough to hide the horses."

Spencer glanced around from his study of Calvo Sotelo, appraised the shaft, then went without another word to get his horse.

Calvo watched them, he and his burro less curious than interested. To the burro it was simply an intrusion where he had never before encountered strangers but to Calvo who had lived all his life along the Mexican border, it meant a lot more than that.

They led their horses inside his mineshaft, with ample overhead clearance and although the horses were not eager to enter, they were too tired to offer more than a token of resistance, then permitted themselves to be led and pushed and pulled until they were inside out of sight.

One of the strangers, the darker one, walked out to Calvo with a smile. "We got a little trouble," he said. "We'll pay you to lend us a hand, *amigo*."

Calvo nodded and stood in silence.

"There are six riders somewhere over yonder," the stranger gestured. "They'll be a few miles back but comin' straight along. And they'll have tracks to follow. We'll pay you to take the burro and drag brush to cover our tracks. But you got to hurry. All right?"

Calvo thought: Six more *gringos* coming into his canyon to discover his secret mine. *That* mattered, not these two who would flee southward as soon as it was safe for them to do so. He nodded his head and the dark-eyed outlaw flagged him away with a gloved hand.

To lead the burro up the scabrous slope took moments. The burro knew every yard of this uphill grade. Above, Calvo looked back but saw nothing. The outlaws were inside his mine with their worn-out saddle animals. Calvo cut faggots, quickly wrapped them and started dragging back and forth, walking ahead of his little animal over the clear marks left by two shod horses.

He did not see the other horsemen until he was more than a mile away, out where shale-rock made tracking harder and the six riders were coursing back and forth moving slowly as they advanced.

Calvo watched with calm eyes. He understood this

sort of thing very well. All his mature life he had either been looking for tracks of one kind or another, or leaving tracks of his own. He was perfectly satisfied, if these other ones were also *gringos,* that he could delude them.

When he turned back he covered his own tracks as well. He also kept to the taller stands of underbrush to avoid being detected as he went back to the rim of his canyon to wait. He had no intention of going back down there until he was convinced those other six would not come over here too. They would be a posse, and if they caught him down there with the two outlaws . . .

He squatted beside his drowsy burro, rolled and lit a cigarette, and listened to every sound which carried almost endlessly in this deathly hushed place with the clear, crystal air.

3
THE WAIT

"Suppose," queried Paul Spencer, "that old Mex sells us out?"

Doria was smoking when he answered. "We are at the end of the road anyway." He smiled from where he was off-saddling his exhausted animal. "And if those six think they can come in here to get us—they'll have to be pretty damned dumb."

"They can starve us out, Jim."

"Yeah. Let's wait until they do it." Doria offered his

thin tobacco sack. "Maybe the old Mex will sell us out, but I don't think so. Anyway, I sure don't want to think so."

The horses drowsed in the cool gloom while their owners shared a smoke, punched back their hats and sat just inside the shaft listening. Even if the old Mex did sell them out, six possemen coming down that loose-rock slope—even if they attempted it on foot, to be cunning—would scatter stones and make noise.

Paul scratched, peered out, wagged his head and said, "There's a real nice little saloon up in the Cache Le Poudre country at a cowtown called Jelm. Just right for a man to run by himself, and set in the shade in summertime and next to his stove in wintertime."

Jim Doria was indifferently interested. "That's what you want to do with your share of the loot? Set around pouring drinks, listening to gossip, and getting fat for the rest of your life?"

Paul gestured. "You think settin' in some old Mex's cave is better?"

"No. But then I don't expect to set here for very long . . . You hear anything?"

Paul leaned and eased ahead until he could see out. "It's the old Mex and his jackass . . . How long we been in here?"

"Couple hours. You see anything else?"

"Nope." Paul pulled back. "You ever been to the town he named?"

"Soledad? No, never have. But I know what the name means—a lonely place in the desert."

"Really? How they get all that into one word? You know very much Spanish?"

Doria leaned to also look over where Calvo Sotelo and his solemn little burro were walking. "I learned how to ask for a drink of water, how to say thank-you, and please, and to say it looks like it might rain." Jim arose and brushed grit from his britches with his hat. "I spent a year in New Mexico one time."

"Yeah, you told me. In jail down there."

They both met Calvo at the entrance. He said, "They went south in the direction of the stageroad."

"Toward the town?"

"*Si*, toward the town." Calvo's calm gaze did not leave them as he forced into words an idea which had occurred to him on the hike back down into the canyon. "They can hire men in Soledad who can read tracks very good . . . They can hire those men to go back there where they lost your sign and read my brush marks. *Señores,* you will have maybe two hours."

Jim Doria did not suspect he and Paul were being deliberately incited to rush away by someone wishing to protect a secret, but he was sure of one thing, so he said, "Partner, these horses aren't going to make it another five miles."

Paul stepped around the burro to look elsewhere, not because he was nervous nor particularly apprehensive, but because it had become his second nature to be wary, especially in strange country.

Calvo considered. It was true that their horses were

used up, but he had to get them away from *Yelmo Cañon*. For the time being they were only interested in avoiding capture and in flight, but if they remained here for a day or two, they would become interested in the old cave—which was not really a cave at all.

Doria abruptly said, "*Señor,* suppose we gave you money to go down to your town, buy two good horses and fetch them back here to us?" He reached into a trouser pocket and drew forth some sweat-flattened greenbacks. He peeled off a big one and smiled. "That's for you brushin' out our sign, *amigo.*" He watched the old Mexican examine the greenback. "That much more if you'll bring us back two strong, sound horses . . . How much will you need to buy them?"

Calvo raised his eyes from the greenback. They had to be complete strangers not to realize a Mexican faggot-gatherer could not appear in any border cow-town with that much money without the law, and everyone else who heard of it, becoming very suspicious as well as very antagonistic. But he pocketed the greenback.

"With fresh horses you can be into Mexico by dawn tomorrow, *Señores.* If you are careful. Those six men will still be out here."

"Yeah. How much more money do you need?"

Calvo shrugged because he did not need any more of those greenbacks of large denominations. In fact one of the worst things which could befall him would for the sheriff at Soledad to find him carrying notes

26

that crisp and new and large. So, he would steal two horses.

"I will get the horses first," he told them.

Paul Spencer, the Montanan who had been in Wyoming and Colorado and knew nothing about Mexicans, had in fact only seen perhaps fifty or sixty of them in his lifetime, stood hipshot while he studied Calvo Sotelo. He was distrustful. He was also a born realist, and neither he nor Jim Doria were going any farther without fresh animals.

Calvo knew the look he was getting. He made no attempt to mitigate it. If he had, if he had told them their secret was absolutely safe with him, then the next question they would ask would be—why?

He faced Doria and repeated it. "I will get the horses and bring them back. Then we will talk about what they cost." He ranged a look up along the rims. "*Señores,* stay out of sight. I will be back in the evening." He turned, spoke to the burro, and walked away herding the little beast ahead of him.

Paul watched them leaving. "I don't trust him. I've heard lots of stories about how treacherous Messicans are."

Doria also stood in the gloom watching Calvo leave. "I trust him. If he'd wanted to sell us out he had the best chance he'll ever have up there on the plain, and he didn't do it."

"Maybe he figures we got a lot of money and he'll sneak back here with a bunch more Messicans in the dark."

Jim's stomach was making sounds so he went back inside to rummage his saddlebags for a couple of tins of salt beef. When Paul joined him in there he said, "You sure you trust him?"

Doria tossed across one of the tins. "Yeah."

"How much money did you give him?"

"Ten dollars. For brushing out the tracks." Jim sat down and went to work with his Barlow knife worrying the tin free of the salt meat. "The first decent town we hit in Mexico I'm going to hunt up a café and eat for a week."

"What do they call cafés in Messico?"

"Damned if I know. I remember that they called saloons *cantinas*. Maybe it's the same for a beanery. These are our last two tins of grub. Did you know that?"

Paul Spencer leaned back to eat with his pocket-knife and for a while had nothing to say. Outside, the shadows lengthened, but up out of the canyon there was still broad daylight.

Doria slept and Paul Spencer went out front to sit in the fading daylight wishing for a smoke while he cradled his Winchester and speculated on what would happen once full twilight came.

Doria was not worried, so *he* would not worry. Doria had a knack for scenting trouble and if he were worried now he would not be sprawling out inside that old cave or whatever it was, sound asleep.

In the cool of pre-evening a fat, stubby rattlesnake crawled forth from the ground-level limbs of a scrub brush to begin his nocturnal foraging.

Any other time Paul would have shot him. Now, he simply sat watching the reptile, and when it scouted up a hole which Paul had not seen before, then sucked back, plunged its head and neck down the hole to scent rodents if there were any, Paul was tempted to walk over there and land on the snake's back with both feet.

The snake pulled back. Evidently there had been no desert mice in that particular hole for a long while. The rattler lifted its head and turned, showing its blunt, shiny snout to Spencer. "You son of a bitch," Paul told the snake, "if you crawl over here I'm going to drop a rock on you."

The snake turned and crawled away, disappearing finally beyond some low bushes with mottled, waxy leaves and Paul stepped over there after a while to make certain the snake hadn't circled around to head for the cave.

Jim came out, spat, went over to drop down and drink, returned and said, "What in hell did you buy salt meat for, when we're down on the desert?"

Paul looked disgusted. "*I* didn't buy that, *you* did. In that little timbered town we passed through four, five days ago . . . Hey, there's a big fat darned snake around here. Don't let him come inside the cave, I'm going to sleep for a little."

Jim tossed over the thin tobacco sack but Paul pitched it back. "I'll wait until we hit a town," he said. "Thanks anyway . . . Mind that darned snake, will you?"

"What was he—a rattler?"

"Yeah, and as thick as your wrist. Short and stubby and thicker'n a tree-limb."

"Greenish?"

"No. Sort of tan-brown with a real ugly face."

Jim grinned. "The green ones are the snakes that'll kill you. They're timber rattlers. Never get very long and they're big around."

Spencer scowled. "I know what a timber rattler looks like. Bettern'n you do . . . What are you tryin' to do, scare me?"

"Naw. Where would you get such an idea? Anyway, you're already scairt. Go on, sleep. I'll kick dirt in his face if he comes around here . . . unless he's one of those real sly ones and figures a way to sneak around me and get inside with you."

Paul turned with a grunt and entered the cave. From in there, when he called back, his voice had two or three hollow-sounding echoes accompanying it. "Hey, Jim; this here is some sort of old mine."

Doria sat down and propped his back against stone. "The only thing I know about mines is that gold comes out of them, and the only time I know gold is when I see it in someone's teeth . . . Hey, I think I just saw your snake. By golly he's big enough to throw a saddle on, and now he's got ten other fellers with him."

"Go to hell!"

The shadows did not seem to darken perceptibly after their initial arrival. The pleasant warmth did not vary five degrees from what it had been at midday.

Jim Doria had a smoke, drank more water, then speculated about those possemen. If, as the old Mex thought, they had gone down to the town south of here, they would surely seek out the marshal or deputy or whatever they had down there, and then the hunt would be on all over again.

Whether those possemen would tell the south desert lawman Doria and Spencer had cleaned out a bank of ten thousand new dollars was problematical. The closer one got to the Mexican border, the greater temptations became, with a badge or without one. But what mattered was that those possemen from up north would be waiting, searching left and right and seeking. Whoever they were, they had abundantly demonstrated that they did not give up easily.

Except for the Mexican with his burro, by now they quite likely would have the money as well as the outlaws who had stolen it.

He finished his smoke, watched a hairy black spider as large as the back of his hand move with incredibly rapid lurching jumps as it emerged for its twilight hunt and when he got close enough he killed time by pitching small pebbles at it. The spider was so fast not a single well-aimed stone came close to it.

Jim flung several stones at once and marveled at the way the big spider could avoid every one of them. Then he lifted his hat, ran a set of bent fingers through his hair, reset the hat and watched the spider soar into the air, a blur of hairy speed, and catch a large flying insect in flight.

He sighed, shifted position a little and looked up along the darkening ridge wondering why anyone in their right mind would deliberately live in country like this.

Paul came out, went wordlessly past to drink at the hollowed-out stone, then came back and sat beside Jim, still without saying a word, and held up his closed fist, then very dramatically opened it.

"You know what that is on my palm?" he asked.

Jim leaned. "Yeah. Some dirty little pieces of rock."

Paul got out his pocketknife and scraped until the small pebbles shone dully. "Look now."

Jim leaned again to humor his partner. They were not going anywhere yet, and there was nothing much else to look at. He raised a finger to push some of the pebbles around, then remained stationary for a long time.

"Gold!"

"Yeah. Now you know why the old Mex didn't sell us out to the possemen. This here is his secret mine."

"Where'd you find that stuff?"

Paul jerked his head. "Back down inside the cave about a hundred yards. It's darker'n the inside of a boot down there. And that shaft goes a hell of a distance back inside that hill we rode down here on."

Doria took several of the little stones and scraped them with his own knife. The harder he scraped the softer they glowed in their yellowish substance. "I'll be damned." He turned to look inside the large opening where the horses were still drowsily standing.

"Is there much of this stuff back down in there?"

They both arose to return to the mine, and from a fair distance a coyote reared back and yapped into the dead-still desert silence as evening began to finally settle, even up across the plain.

They used all their sulphur matches scratching around in there, and found only a few more pea-sized nuggets along with some thin flakes of gold.

After the first surprise had passed Jim Doria led the way back out front where he utilized the last fading daylight to scratch dirt off more gold. Then he shook his head. "If this is how folks get this stuff, no wonder it's so valuable. A man could wear out his pocketknife in there without getting more than half a tobacco-sack full of it."

Paul leaned to look as he replied. "You got enough gold in your hand to buy six new pocketknives." He straightened back. "And you gave that old Mex ten dollars like you were Santa Claus."

Jim Doria scraped a little more, then put up his knife. "Now I understand why the old cuss was willing to find us a pair of fresh horses. To get us the hell away from his gold mine."

"Yeah. Maybe just far enough away so's he can bushwack us, then there won't be anyone who knows what we know about his mine."

Jim pocketed the tiny bits of gold. "He'd ought to be showing up soon."

"You want to talk to him about his mine?"

Jim looked irritated. "Hell no. We'll leave things as

they are. What *he* don't know and what he thinks *we* don't know won't get anyone in trouble. What we've got to do first, is get away from that darned posse. Maybe later on we can come back here and help the old gent work his mine."

Paul raised his head because he thought he had detected a distant sound. "Yeah. I can picture that Messican handin' over half this mine to us . . . Did you hear anything just now?"

"No. Look yonder. Did you ever see anything like that?"

Paul squinted in the gloom. "What is it?"

"It's a spider as big as your fist."

"A what?"

"Just watch now. It'll jump again."

"By gawd . . . What kind of damned country is this anyway. That's the biggest spider in the world . . . Let's just let the old Mex have his mine and get the hell away from here!"

4
A SURPRISE

They were both grays, the worst possible color of a horse for men to ride who wished to blend into the scenery. They were in their prime, maybe six or seven years old, with large feet and thick, strong legs to go with their short backs and powerful rumps.

Paul Spencer felt like shaking his head but he instead looked at their good points as Calvo Sotelo dismounted from one of them and stood holding the shank to the second gray horse.

Jim Doria studied them in silence, briefly, then said, "How much money, *amigo?*"

Calvo's answer was quietly offered. "Nothing—*amigo*—I stole them."

That made Paul say, "There'll be a damned posse then."

Calvo shrugged and handed Jim the lead-shanks. "No. Not today and maybe not even tomorrow. I stole them from a remuda some cowmen had turned loose a few days ago. *Señores,* I am a poor man. If I had bought two good horses and paid for them in cash . . . Soledad is a small place. Everyone knows everyone else's business . . . you understand?"

Doria was placating. "Sure, we understand. We want to pay you for the risk you ran, anyway. And for helpin' us." He reached in his pocket but Calvo shook his head.

"Those six men are in town. They were at the café with the deputy sheriff. Their leader is named Carter Alvarado. We know him down here. Get on the gray horses, *Señores,* and don't get off for twenty miles, until you are in *Chihuahua.*"

Doria's gaze turned speculative. "Who is Carter Alvarado?"

"*Pistolero,*" replied Calvo. "A very bad man. A manhunter. People say he has never failed to get someone he goes after. Those men with him . . ." Calvo softly frowned. "Bad. I don't know any of them

35

but I know men, and those five are just as bad as Carter Alvarado."

"Does your deputy know this Alvarado?"

"*Si*. Everyone knows Alvarado. He is known throughout all New Mexico."

Paul Spencer groaned. "Nice, Jim. You got to give us credit, when we get someone after us it's no penny-ante town constable . . . And that answers the question about who they were and how come them never to slack off. Professional manhunters. Hey mister, does this Alvarado live up north in a place called Rosario?"

Calvo had no idea about that so he said, "Anywhere. Men like that live anywhere."

Paul turned back to studying the patient-standing pair of grays. Jim Doria smiled at Calvo. "We're obliged to you, partner."

Sotelo woodenly nodded. "You are wasting time, *Señores*."

Doria went into the mine to get his outfit and drag it out where he could throw it upon one of the grays. Paul followed this example, while Calvo Sotelo stood aside watching.

There was a two-thirds moon, lopsided and rusty colored, to accompany the pleasant desert warmth. Down in the canyon it was less dark, now that there was moonlight and starshine, than it had been earlier.

They checked their new horses because they knew nothing whatsoever about them, then swung up and settled for a moment of waiting, but neither gray so much as humped beneath the saddle.

Calvo pointed to a low place in the rims without saying a word. Paul nodded curtly and reined around but Jim Doria leaned to extend a hand. "Whatever your reason for helping, it don't matter, mister. We're downright grateful."

Calvo stood in the darkness, a gaunt baggy wraith in ill-fitting white blouse and trousers, watching as the outlaws headed southward. Then he went over to the mineshaft, produced a candle from inside his blouse, lit it and went slowly back and forth examining the walls. When he was satisfied he returned to the entrance and stood for a moment gazing out where there was no longer a sign of the outlaws, and swore softly. He had found several places where someone had scratched with a pocketknife. Well; the thing to hope for now was that the outlaws escaped down into Mexico and would not return. Maybe ever, although men of that kind did not forget.

Something up the northwesterly slope moved, and started a rattling small avalanche. The noise carried. Calvo spun to see, but it was too dark up there. Perhaps a fox or a coyote. He did not have a weapon, but the longer he stood waiting the less it appeared he might need one; no more sounds came from up there.

He waited a full hour and still there was no indication that he was not alone, so he finally went trudging homeward. It was a lengthy walk but he had been walking most of his life. He needed the solitude for thinking.

For no reason he knew of, Fate was doing this to

him; was sending *pistoleros* into his life. Not just the running men, but Alvarado and the deputy in Soledad, Mike Curtis, a burly, thick-bodied Missourian with coarse features and a distrust of Mexicans.

The night was pleasant, which meant full summer was approaching. It was easy to walk southward because the land was flat in that direction, and no one would meet him, even when he got back to town because he knew ways of approaching his adobe house without attracting attention.

A pair of owls exchanged calls and once as he skirted around a low, thick bush some little animal bounded forth in complete surprise, then fled in a swift pattern of zigzagging rushes.

He detected the aroma of Soledad while still a fair distance out. People had finished supper, even among the *jacals* of Mex-town, but the fragrance lingered to remind Calvo he had not had much to eat this day.

A dog barked, naturally. That was one thing no one had devised a satisfactory defense against, but fortunately not many people heeded barking dogs. Other dogs joined in, but that tended to annoy people rather than to alert them so he got back to town without difficulty.

He did not go directly to his adobe house. He went first to the stoned-in compound where his burros stayed, to make certain they had water and feed, then he went over to the large patch of vegetables he and several other older men maintained out behind the dilapidated old adobe church. It did no harm to help feed the priest, a large man with pale eyes, hair the shade of new carrots, who spoke Spanish and Latin with a New York accent.

Finally he turned toward his adobe residence. The town was quiet, even over along the main thoroughfare where a *gringo* saloon at this time of year, when the cowmen were drifting in their north-country herds, commonly remained busy until very late.

He came around the side of his house to the meager porch with its dilapidated thatched overhang and paused a moment in the cool late night to consider how this day had gone, then went indoors to bed.

In Mex-town people retired later, as a general rule. In *gringo* town, which had the backs of its stores and sheds to the old town, people had early supper and retired early. It was Mexican custom to sleep in the hottest part of each afternoon even when it was not all that hot, then to arise about the time the *Norteamericanos* were getting ready to go home for supper. The Mexicans ate about eight or nine o'clock, which was about the time the *gringos* were climbing into bed. Nor did the residents of Mex-town retire for the night until perhaps ten or eleven, sometimes not until midnight, and sometimes, as with the lean wraith who watched everything Calvo Sotelo did after his return to town, they had some business which kept them up until much later.

The wraith lingered long after Calvo's candle had been snuffed out, then it drifted to the stone corral and probed all the places where Calvo had been, under the somber gaze of both burros. Finally, the wraith returned to the area of Calvo's rude small house and hovered like an avenging angel, sometimes appearing ready to enter, other times giving the distinct impression of someone who would *like* to enter, other times giving the distinct impression of someone who would *like* to enter but who for some reason feared to do so.

Then the thin, wiry silhouette vanished eastward out through Mex-town.

These bland nights were not uncommon in summertime, but this was still springtime. Summer was weeks away. Usually, there was a chill to each late night this time of year. Especially as time worked along toward dawn.

Tonight was an exception. Last night had also been an exception and to knowledgeable desert-dwellers, if they were awake at all, this phenomenon would have suggested rain in the offing.

But by morning the sky was just as flawless as it had been for the past week and more. If there were rain clouds they were beyond the horizon.

To Paul Spencer these were typical desert nights. Even to Doria they appeared as typical and he perhaps should have known better, having been down through here a couple of times before.

But since they were personally concerned with hunger, not the delicate, pleasant warm beauty of a fragile south desert dawn, the unusual warmth eluded them.

They had been discussing what they *should* have done. Paul thought they should have got food at that town back yonder, the place called Soledad, which they had passed along the east side, looking and listening as they soundlessly moved along.

Jim thought they should have stopped on the outskirts, or maybe in Mex-town, and purchased food. Now, he was of the opinion they should seek a cow-camp and either watch until the riders were gone, or simply ride in and using guns take food. He did not believe they should push the balance of the distance over the line down into the province of Chihuahua, without strengthening themselves, for while they now had fresh, strong horses under them, *they* were the weak ones now.

Paul gestured. "All right. Where is a cow-camp?"

If there had been one within a half mile they would not have been able to see it because the sun did not arrive for a half hour after they had passed well south of Soledad.

"Patience," admonished Jim Doria.

Paul looked around. "You know, this is a hell of a way for wealthy men to be—with money bustin' the seams of their saddlebags—and shrunken guts."

"It goes with our trade," replied Doria. "My daddy used to say that if a man don't take a risk now and then he don't gain much."

"What did he say about missing meals all the time?"

"Probably nothing, because he didn't miss any that I knew of." Jim Doria replied, then casually raised a

41

hand to point. "Cattle. Somewhere around here is a cow-camp."

The animals were lean, probably from having wintered in the northerly country, and from also having been driven to the south desert within the past week or two, but they were good livestock, the kind cattlemen kept after all the culling was done. They were also wary; the moment they saw riders in the low glow of early dawn, they stopped dead-still and watched, heads high ready to run.

Neither Doria nor Spencer could make out brands, as much because they could not get close enough as because of the poor light, which was probably just as well because they happened to be riding horses bearing the same marks.

Some trees loomed ahead as daylight brightened. The horsemen angled in that direction expecting to find water, which they came upon where someone a long while back had developed a weak spring and had siphoned the trickle through wooden pipe to a huge stone trough which had been built at great expense in labor, but built well. Even now, perhaps two generations later, there was scarcely any leakage.

Doria piled off, yanked loose his saddle and bridle to allow the gray horse to get down and roll, then to drink and amble over where some short sawgrass grew along the course of the spring's slight overflow.

Spencer did the same, then he too drank, and swore because the water had a faint sulphur taste.

The sun was above its easternmost bulwarks

flooding the empty land with golden brilliance. There were small birds busily working throughout the coarse underbrush on all sides, and except for their little piping chatter the desert was silent.

Doria hauled his outfit over beyond the tall old shaggy trees, dumped it there and sank down to close his eyes for a brief nap while the horses browsed. When Spencer came over, also dragging his outfit, he said, "Now, which would you like for breakfast, a thick stack of flapjacks smothered in syrup, or a lean steak fried with spuds and washed down with a half gallon of new coffee?"

Doria opened his eyes. "What I'd like would be a partner who had been born mute."

As he dropped down Spencer groaned. "Gratitude! This world is full of folks without any gratitude."

"It's full of something," conceded Jim Doria, "but I'm not sure it's a lack of gratitude."

The warmth increased a few degrees at a time. The men became drowsy. Those little birds must have hurried along, or else perhaps they had burrowed deeper into the underbrush to roost, but at any rate they were no longer making their busy little shrill sounds. In fact the silence deepened steadily until it would have been possible to hear a pocket-watch ticking, if either Doria or Spencer owned a pocket-watch.

Then a horse whinnied. Both outlaws spun around from over behind their big old shaggy trees, guns rising from hip-holsters in a blur of speed.

A man's rough profanity came through the warming

daylight, then a shout. "Hey, Max! Here are the grays by gawd!"

Four horsemen appeared from through the under-brush. A fifth man sat with both hands atop his sad-dlehorn gazing ahead where the grays were eating. "How the hell did they get this far east?" he growled. Then he gestured. "Get in behind them and let's get back to camp. The old man'll quit storming around for a change. He was so damned sure Mex horsethieves had got them."

Spencer and Doria lay hidden by the mottled shade of the old trees, watching those cowboys swoop around behind the stolen horses and turn them in a flinging gallop. Moments later when even the dimin-ishing sound of running horses had died away, Spencer sat up, leathered his six-gun, and said, "Well, here we sit with ten thousand dollars an' we can't even buy a tin of beans with it—and now we're on foot."

Doria said nothing as he re-holstered his gun and lifted his hat to scratch.

Spencer looked one last time in the direction of the rangemen. "Now—we're on foot, and what I'd like to know is—which is closest, Soledad back yonder, or some Mex town on southward."

Jim said, "Soledad. We're still a few miles from the border, and there aren't any towns closer than maybe another eight or ten miles below the line."

"You sure?"

"No. But I'm sure of one thing: we *know* where Soledad is."

44

Spencer arose and beat dust off himself, then gazed at their saddlery. "Soledad by my guess is ten miles north. My saddle weighs forty pounds without the blanket, bridle and saddlebags. I'm not going to pack it any ten miles."

They rigged lariat ropes in the tree-limbs and hoisted both saddles up where rodents and other varmints would not be able to eat the leather for the salt-sweat in it. Then they buried the saddlebags containing their stolen wealth. By that time the heat was increasing to a point where it was more noticeable than it had been the day before. Also, there were several veil-like layers of high mistiness. This added somewhat to the heat for some obscure reason.

Both men tanked up at the trough then wordlessly turned to trudge back in the direction from which they had come during the previous night. They walked for a mile or two with little conversation. Paul Spencer finally said, "I don't think I want to stay in this business. We haven't been caught yet, true enough, but for a darned fact if we'd stayed at working the cow ranges we wouldn't have any money but we sure as hell wouldn't be on foot in the middle of a desert, neither."

Doria nodded. "And suppose some varmint digs up those saddlebags and gnaws up our money?"

"I'll chuck the whole business and maybe go to freighting."

Doria frowned. "Not freighting, for gosh sakes. Nobody goes to freighting unless they got no self-respect."

"Then I'll open a blacksmith shop in some nice little town."

"Naw. It's too hard on a man's back."

"What then?"

Doria mopped sweat before answering. "Something where a man can sit down a lot. Maybe driving stages."

"Are you crazy? There's always some lawless bastard robbing stagecoaches."

5
TROUBLE

Soledad was like a graveyard when they finally got back up there.

Neither of them knew the town but it was very little different from other towns of its size so they had no difficulty in getting the feel of the place, and they had one stroke of good fortune, they found an unlocked cooler-house out back of an old adobe building which had probably at one time been a barracks and which was now the local boarding-house. The cooler-house had rows of bottled peaches and apples and plums, along with tins of canned meat.

They ate out behind the old adobe building without attracting even any of the local dogs, had a smoke, and sat for an hour or so recuperating from their unaccustomed hike, then went in search of two horses to steal, and while the public corrals or the liverybarn were the most reasonable places to accomplish their purpose, the public corrals were empty and there were two nightmen playing blackjack by a smoky old overhead lamp in the liverybarn runway.

Jim was of the opinion they might do better over in Mex-town so they skirted around in that direction as soundless and shapeless as shadows. There were a number of faggot corrals over there, all of which were close to local *jackals*. Too close in most cases for health; all a horse had to do was snort at the scent of two strangers to awaken some light-sleeping Mexican, and even in the dark at such close range someone with a gun could scarcely miss. But they found one adobe residence which seemed to possess about three rooms, and which had a goat pen along with a stoned-in burro corral where not only were there several horses standing tied nearby, but they were saddled and bridled.

Paul Spencer hung back with justifiable wariness. No one left that many horses tied this late at night, saddled and ready to ride, unless they were inside the *jacal* dressed and prepared to ride out.

Jim Doria stood in darkness eyeing the horses. They were lean animals, but tough and serviceable. "Poker session," he opined. "Or maybe an all-night game of pedro."

Spencer scowled. "Pedro?"

"Yeah. It's a card game Mexicans play a lot."

Spencer pointed. "In the damned dark?"

It was a good observation. The house was dark.

Doria lightly scratched the tip of his nose, then

wordlessly slipped ahead until he was close enough to get a closer view of the horses. He was more interested in them than the houses, but he nonetheless remained well clear of the two small, glassless windows as he skirted up to one corner of the house, then edged around it in the direction of the rack where the horses were.

A man groaned, and after an interval of silence he groaned again. Doria flattened along the wall. Moments later someone gruffly said, "Shut up. You aren't dead yet. A couple of punches don't hurt that much."

The groaning man was briefly silent, then he groaned again and this time a different voice, higher and more distinct, said, "You son of a bitch I'm goin' to give you something to groan about if you don't quit that."

Doria heard a lightly accented voice say, "*Señores,* there is no store of gold at the mine. I told you. I said to your friends there are only those little veins in the walls."

"Yeah," replied the high, distinct voice, "We know what you *said,* but that feller who give us the information said you been goin' and comin' from up there for a long time, so we know you got it hid. And I'll tell you something else, pepperbelly, if our friends don't find it, you're goin' to wish to hell they had!"

Doria momentarily forgot the horses. He had recognized the faintly accented voice. After a moment he turned and went back the way he had come.

Spencer was leaning in darkness next to a walled-in spring when his partner returned to report. "There are a couple of fellers inside the house, and they got that old Mexican who helped us. They know about his mine and it sounded to me like they beat hell out of him to find his cache."

Spencer turned from his study of the tethered horses. "You sure it's the same old Mex?"

"I didn't see him in there but it sure sounded like his voice. And how many Mexicans around here got secret mines? Paul, the old guy did us some favors."

Spencer turned to range a look along the front of the adobe house. "Two of them inside? There are three horses over there."

Doria had only heard two men. "One more shouldn't make much difference," he said, "if we can get the drop on 'em."

Spencer straightened up. "Let's go," he said, and started forward using the same route his partner had used to get around behind the house.

Once, they had to drop flat. A man stepped out of the *jacal* to look around, to expectorate, to gaze at the tethered horses briefly, then turn and re-enter the house.

Doria said, *"Gringo."*

Spencer said nothing, he got back to his feet, brushed off dust and walked on over to the back of the house, leaned there until Doria came up, then strained to hear noises inside, but there were none. As he straightened back he said, "We can cut the horses loose, which ought to bring them out of there."

Doria shook his head. "We might need those horses. Two of them anyway." He pointed to one of the glassless little windows set in the thick wall. "I'll get under that thing. You get around by the door. I'll raise up and cover them from the window. You get the doorway."

"How you goin' to cover 'em when it's dark in there?"

Doria was tugging loose the tie-down on his holstered six-gun when he answered. "They won't be able to see any better than we can, and they're exposed inside while we got three feet of adobe mud in front of us . . . You got a better idea?"

"Call 'em out," said Spencer, and at the pained look he got he started to turn away as he said, "All right. I'll mind the door. If this works I'll eat my hat."

Jim Doria grinned. He had sore feet and sore ankles, but at least his stomach was full, and with a man of his toughness that more than compensated for other small irritations.

He slipped around to the window, got below it, squatted there until he was sure his partner was at the door, then very slowly raised up.

There was one feeble candle on a table inside the *jacal*. Its light radiated less than fifteen feet but since the room was even smaller, it cast an adequate amount of light for Doria to make out the bound form of a man on the earthen floor, and two other men at the table, seated.

He lifted his Colt slowly, rested it across the sill,

which was two feet thick, and something, perhaps a whisper of sound as the gun settled, or an instinct, made the man facing the window raise his eyes. There were some scattered playing cards lying in front of him. He did not touch them. He did not in fact seem able to breathe.

The second man was facing the door, his left side to the window and he was scooping up the cards and muttering something indistinguishable as though he were disgusted about something. If there was a third man he was not in the little room. At least he was not at the table nor immediately visible to Doria. A sudden, sharp command quietly from just beyond the doorway as someone said, "Hold it! Right there!" sounded like Spencer.

The man picking up cards hauled straight up and began to twist to look. His partner spoke gently. "Mike! Don't do it! Look at the winder."

The moving man let the cards drop from his hand and turned swiftly until he too was staring at the cocked Colt atop the recessed windowsill.

Outside front of the house Doria heard his partner say, "Face the wall, mister. *Face it!*"

For five seconds there was not a sound, then Doria motioned for the seated men to arise. "Drop the guns," he told them. "Be careful, fellers. Be gawddamn careful." While watching the two strangers obey he raised his voice slightly. "Paul; you get one?"

Instead of replying Spencer gave the stranger he had disarmed a rough push into the room and came in directly behind the man. "I guess I got to eat my hat," he mumbled. "Come on in, Jim. We got enough hands for a session of poker."

Doria went to the door and stood there waiting for his partner to go over the strangers for hideouts. When Spencer was satisfied Doria watched Spencer kneel to free Calvo Sotelo and help him to a rude little wall-bunk.

The Mexican studied his rescuers, then dolefully wagged his head. "You shouldn't have come back," he said. "These are three of Alvarado's riders."

One of the unarmed men lifted his eyes quickly to stare. Then he said, "Spencer and Doria!" The other two riders took fresh interest. One of them, a large, thick man with a lipless, twisted mouth and a very thick-bridged nose which pushed his eyes too far apart, made a slow, sneering smile. "The old greaser's right. You boys shouldn't have showed up."

Doria replied matter-of-factly. "Didn't have any choice . . . Where's the other three?"

None of the captives would answer but Sotelo did. "They are out at my mine."

"How did they know you had a mine?" asked Paul Spencer.

Sotelo's disconsolate expression deepened a little in the weak light of that solitary candle. "I have a neighbor named Garcia. A nosy, sneaking man. He has been watching me go and come for a long time. He told them when the deputy sheriff came for him. Garcia is the Mex-town spy for Deputy Curtis . . . I know Garcia very well. I never thought he would be able to guess about me or the mine. But he guessed. He spied on me last night. When I came back, these men came—only there were six of them including Carter Alvarado."

Doria gazed at the slumped old man. "And they knocked it out of you about the mine?"

"*Si.* Alvarado and the other two rode up there to find where I hid the gold."

Spencer considered the sneering, thick man with the ox-eyes, who appeared the most likely to use violence. "You hit the old gent, did you, mister?"

The big man's sneer lingered. "I had a little talk with him," he conceded, and although he probably had surmised where this conversation might lead, he had no way of knowing how fast Spencer was. The fist came so abruptly the big man had no chance to twist away. It sounded like a sledgehammer going into meat, the way the blow landed with all its force up alongside the big posseman's head. The man dropped, took a little wooden bench with him over backward, landed on his side and did not move, but the other two moved simultaneously and regardless of Doria's gun. They both went after Paul Spencer. One of them swung haymakers, like a windmill, as he swore and sprang in. Spencer was struck twice, once in the middle of the chest and the second time on the shoulder, high enough to wrench him half around.

He stepped back and curved away as Doria went ahead, holstering his Colt with one hand as he reached to grab cloth and wrench one of the men around to face him. He aimed perfectly. The posseman went to his knees from a strike on the jaw, and when Doria leaned to haul him back up right, the posseman tried clumsily to turn away, but he had been stunned. The second blow put him flat down.

Spencer's engagement with the one who waded in like a windmill was brief too. He half-circled, watched until both the man's big arms were high and distant from the man's unprotected body, then he sank low and buried one fist to the wrist in yielding flesh, then straightened the man up with his second blow. The man crumpled with a gasp.

Spencer straightened up, looked at the three men on the earthen floor, looked at his partner, and then systematically went over to flop each posseman face-down and rummage for wallets.

Jim Doria went across to sink down upon the bunk beside Calvo Sotelo. "Mister, the outfit you got those gray horses from caught us down-country restin' in the shade, and ran off their horses. So we came back." He flexed his right hand and gazed at his partner who was counting the greenbacks he had taken from the inert possemen. "How much?"

"Sixty dollars." Spencer pocketed the money and gingerly probed the side of his face where one of those windmill blows had grazed upwards. "Oldtimer, you better get hold of that feller named Garcia and fix his wagon for him."

Calvo raised his eyes. "What of these men," he said,

waving one hand. "And the other three? Now they know."

"Did you have some gold cached up there at the mine?"

"No. But it might have been better if I'd had some out there. When Alvarado returns . . ."

Spencer understood. "Yeah. He'll want to cut your throat. Mister, it's not goin' to be a secret any more. You'd be better off to take the third horse out front and ride south with us."

Calvo shook his head. "I can't go down into Mexico."

Doria and Spencer stared. One of them said, "You're wanted in Mexico?"

Calvo Sotelo considered his answer and offered it reluctantly. "Years ago I heard of a raid being planned by brigands down there and warned the army up here. The army set up an ambush . . . They had a price on my head for ten years. They would remember even yet."

Doria stood up, stepped to the door and looked around, out in the cooling night, then he turned and said, "You'd better at least hide out until these possemen leave, mister."

But Calvo was disconsolate about that as well. "The deputy sheriff here in Soledad—he knows about the mine too. Garcia had told him. If I leave I can never return."

"It's better'n being dead isn't it?" asked Spencer. "This Alvarado seems to be a tough man to get clear of. And if they figure your mine's worth anything you won't be the first feller got buried over a mine."

From the doorway Doria had another question. "How long have the others been out there?"

"Time enough to get back, *Señores*. I thought it was them when you came." Calvo arose and steadied himself for a moment then said, "*Señores,* the deputy is with them."

Spencer sighed and rubbed the sore knuckles of his right hand. "We'd better be moving, gents, unless we figure to hang around here and get into more trouble."

Doria was willing except for one thing. "That bastard Alvarado's never going to let up, Paul. After what we did here, he's going to be worse after us than ever."

Spencer began to scowl. "Here comes another of your ideas."

"We can settle his hash right here, tonight. He don't know we're here. If we light out on fresh horses he's going to come after us again, six strong like before, and maybe even with a posse from here as well as their deputy. Now, we got smaller odds. Tomorrow, the odds'll be at least three to one again and likely closer to six to one."

Spencer stopped massaging his swelling hand and flexed the knuckles as he said, "You're going to get us killed. That's what you're goin' to do."

6
A MATTER OF CONSCIENCE

They stepped outside to smoke and briefly talk. Doria said they had to take Calvo Sotelo with them and Spencer said the Mexican would not go with them, and even if he did, they could not take him down into Mexico, and if they left him alone Alvarado's men would track him down.

"We might just as well settle this thing right here," Spencer exclaimed.

Doria scowled. "How?"

Spencer smiled. "I don't know. You're the one who is forever thinkin' up ways and means. Well, think of something now."

They went back indoors. One of the possemen was moaning and beginning to feebly move. Doria stepped across to the man, yanked loose a trouser-belt and the shellbelt, bound the man's arms behind his back and lashed his ankles, then he propped the man along the wall and smiled at him. "How'd you fellers know our names?" he asked mildly.

The posseman was no longer in a defiant mood. "We was in Rosario when you and Spencer raided the bank. We didn't know who you was until after the raid and the sheriff up there showed the folks at the bank a bunch of dodgers. They picked out your faces from the lot." The posseman wiggled to get more comfortable. "There's a thousand dollars on each of you.

Carter said it would be a quick way to make wages, so we come after you . . . You got a smoke?"

Doria rummaged the pockets of the other two possemen until he found the makings, then made two cigarettes, one for the tied man, one for himself. He lighted both smokes and said, "How come the deputy to tell Alvarado this old Mex had a cache?"

"He didn't tell him that. He simply told us his informer knew there was an old-time mine up yonder and that this old beaner had been sneakin' back and forth for years."

"Then why did Alvarado go up there?"

"Because we couldn't find no cache down here and Carter figured it'd be up at the mine . . . They worked that old Mex over pretty hard."

"You travel with delightful companions," stated Doria quietly. "How's come Carter left you fellers behind instead of the other three?"

"He just took the fellers nearest to him while he was settin' our saddles, and sent us to make sure Sotelo— that's the Messican—didn't try and get help."

Spencer had been talking with Calvo, had been trying to persuade him to pull out, either with Doria and Spencer or by himself. He had no luck. Calvo Sotelo would agree with everything Spencer said right up to the place where Spencer mentioned leaving Soledad, then Calvo would refuse.

Paul gave it up and came over to where Doria was talking with the posseman. "We're stuck," he said, "unless we tie the old cuss on a horse and make him come with us, at least a long way from Soledad, if he won't go below the border."

The posseman looked up. "Won't make no difference where you and him go, Alvarado won't let up for one minute. He'll ride you down. He always has ridden 'em down."

Doria stood up, considered the tip of his cigarette, then stepped over to utilize the belts of the other two possemen to bind them, then he said, "Paul, let's get the hell on our way." He faced Calvo then. "It's up to you, partner, but if you stay they're goin' to skin you alive."

Sotelo looked up nodding his head. "I have a daughter here, *Señores,* and three grandchildren . . . My *life* is here."

Doria turned. "Paul . . ."

Spencer re-set his hat and followed his partner out into the night where the three sleeping horses were standing.

They did not say a word as they freed two of the horses, snugged up the saddles, turned the animals and swung up. There was a chill to the night as they started quietly around through Mex-town.

A dog appeared, but despite his mature size he was a pup so instead of rushing forth giving tongue, he trotted along grinning and wagging a long bony tail. They spoke to him, and reached the lower end of town.

Spencer suddenly reined up. "The old Mex—he took a hell of a chance for us, Jim."

Doria halted, looked around at the darkened buildings, looked back and said, "He won't leave. What do we do—tie him and force him to come along?"

"Naw. We just set and wait, and when Alvarado and the deputy ride in—we get their attention a little."

"*Five* of them?

Spencer smiled in the gloom. "You figured it was all right to jump 'em inside the house when there was three of 'em."

Doria said, "Crazy as a pet 'coon. It won't work. You mean—waylay 'em at the old Mex's house?"

Paul hadn't planned things to that extent so all he said was, "I figure it's pretty mean to go off and leave the old Mex there after we roughed up his gaolers. Sure as hell they're goin' to be mad as hell—all of them."

"Anything is better'n settin here until dawn," grumped Jim Doria. "All right. But it won't work."

"What won't work?" asked Spencer, turning his horse. "We don't even know yet what we're goin' to do."

"Crazy," muttered Doria, also turning back.

But they did not reach the Sotelo adobe. Several dogs began barking up in that direction. Spencer drew rein. "Alvarado is back," he said.

"Hell's going to bust loose any minute," conceded Doria. "We stole two of their mounts and knocked their friends around a little."

They turned west and avoided a number of buildings to reach the opposite side of town. Over there, they left the horses inside someone's buggy shed where there was fresh hay in a manger, then they went back across through the main part of town on foot, interested to see what would be happening at the Sotelo adobe.

But they had made a miscalculation, those barking dogs over in Mex-town had been responding to the scent of a prowling coyote, not riders.

There had been horsemen though. They simply had not been arriving in town through Mex-town, they had instead returned down the main thoroughfare and had swung off out in front of the jailhouse, four or five of them.

Doria was in a narrow dog-trot between two buildings when he saw the riders come down the road, silent and strung out. He caught his partner's attention and pointed.

They watched as the riders swung off, tied up and walked into the jailhouse. Moments later someone lighted a lamp. Doria made a little clucking sound. "Three hours ago we couldn't get a horse, now they're all over the place."

"Horses hell," mumbled Spencer. "Why didn't they go back to the Sotelo place?"

Doria had no answer. He leaned, studying the tie-rack, then the lighted barred small windows of the deputy's office. He said, "Let's go," and led off back across the empty roadway.

But the walls were too thick for anything to be heard through them. All they could ascertain was that the men were in there. Occasionally a voice would rise slightly, but none of the words were distinguishable.

Spencer shook his head. "They'll go over there directly. We got to get the old Mex out of there."

Doria was willing. One thing he was certain about was that by now Alvarado, the riders with him and the deputy sheriff, knew someone beside the old Mexican had been up there at the mine. Even if their abandoned horses were no longer up there, their tracks would be, along with the boot-tracks of Doria and Spencer. As he followed Spencer back across the roadway and down through that same dog-trot into Mex-town, he decided that without their advantage of surprise they were walking the thin edge of disaster. It would require more than simply darkness to extricate them, and by now their enemies back yonder at the jailhouse were aware that the old Mex hadn't been alone at his mine.

With Alvarado's inherent suspicions, he would have guessed who had been hiding at the mine. They were half way to the *jacal* when Doria said, "We're on thin ice, Paul. We got to get out of here soon."

Spencer did not respond. He halted where they could see the Sotelo house, paused as though to sniff the air, then began a circuitous advance.

One saddled horse was still at the rack out front. It must have been sleeping because it did not raise its head as two shadows crept around the building, and halted where they could hear men talking.

The conversation stopped when Doria and Spencer got close enough to listen, and did not commence again until Spencer was under the outside window, the same window where Doria had stood with his six-gun, then all that was said was a profane reference to Calvo Sotelo being gone, and a bitter comment.

"He's goin' to have to grow wings to keep me from settling with him . . . And it was right under our darned noses, nine tobacco sacks of it."

A third voice, calmer, more matter-of-fact than the other two voices, said, "I told Carter. I kept tryin' to tell him the Messican'd keep his gold where he could have an eye on it, not up at that damned mine. I kept tellin' him."

For a moment there was nothing more said, but as Spencer twisted to look back at Doria, the bitter-sounding man spoke again. "I'm goin' to get that old bastard if it's the last thing I ever do. Him, and Doria and Spencer."

The calm man made a dry remark. "Not unless Carter and that deputy get back here soon. Doria and Spencer will be over the line into Mexico and the old goat-herder will be plumb out of the country."

"Like hell he will. He headed straight for that mine and I'll lay you my share of the bounty money on that!"

Doria tapped his partner's shoulder then turned to silently pass around behind the house where there were no windows. When he halted he said. "You reckon Sotelo really went up there to the mine?"

Spencer's answer was curt. "If he isn't here he sure went *somewhere,* and that's the first smart thing he's

63

done so far. But it better not be back to the mine. They'll get him if he did."

Doria sighed. "If he went somewhere else to hide out, I'd say it'd be our turn to light out . . . But . . ."

"Yeah," grumbled Paul Spencer. "But—if the old goat went up there, then we'd better go up there and warn him, and do you know what we'll be doing if we ride up there too?"

Doria nodded. "Gettin' in a little deeper, and it won't be dark much longer."

"We'll be diggin our own graves," growled Spencer, then stood gazing at his partner briefly before he cursed, then said, "Let's go."

They headed back to the shed where they had left their stolen horses. That light at the jailhouse was still burning and those saddled horses were still tied out front. Jim Doria couldn't quite make sense of that, but he did not comment until they were in the saddle riding silently northward in the direction of the mine.

"Why in hell don't Alvarado and the deputy go over to Sotelo's house to find the men they left there?"

Spencer offered a blunt suggestion. "Because they're divvying up some gold they found at the mine."

Doria was interested. "You reckon? The old Mex had more tobacco sacks of the stuff hidden around?"

Spencer groaned. "I was being sarcastic."

They did not notice a very pale, inches-wide flare of new-day light beginning to firm up over along the

64

eastern horizon as they sashayed their way back and forth through desert underbrush. Daylight was indeed not very far off, and that would increase their peril a hundredfold.

7
ARMADILLOS

Calvo was waiting. He had heard them coming and was to one side of the mineshaft with an old hawg-leg six-shooter which had a twelve-inch barrel. They halted and sat their saddles looking at him with owlish expressions when he stepped forth with the old six-gun levelled.

Spencer said, "You got any bullets in that thing?"

Calvo lowered the gun. "Why did you come up here?" he asked. "Now, they are between you and the border."

"Yeah, well, the fact of the matter is," said Spencer, "we came back for you." He looked around. "You *walked* up here?" Without awaiting a reply Spencer loudly groaned. "Mister, sometimes I don't figure you got a lick of sense. They can run you down as easy as fallin' off a log; you on foot, them on horseback."

"Are they coming?" asked Sotelo.

Spencer shrugged. "Not right behind us, but you can bet a sack of gold they'll be along. And look yonder— daylight's coming."

Doria leaned low to peer inside the tunnel. "Our horses still around here?" he asked, evidently thinking

Calvo could ride away on one of them, but Sotelo shook his head. "I sent them eastward where there is some grass and brush."

Doria straightened up slowly. "Sure you did," he mumbled. "Nothing else has been done right tonight, so that might as well be done wrong too. Now we got to carry you away from here behind one of our saddles."

"*Señores,* I will stay," said the Mexican, drawing himself up. He gestured with his free hand. "If you ride east for six miles you will come to a deep arroyo. You can ride southward down it and no one can see you from above. It will take you within three or four miles of the border."

Spencer leaned with both hands atop the stolen saddle. "Listen—*Señor*—you dug up some sacks of gold at the house, and those three fellers we left there saw you do it. And Alvarado as well as your township deputy know you got some gold. They're going to run you down, take your gold and bust your skull like it was a punky melon."

Calvo listened without interruption but before Spencer had finished he was shaking his head as he had done before. "They won't find me," he stated with conviction. "If I don't want to be found out here, no one can find me. As for the sacks of gold," he twisted to point in the direction of the tunnel. "I left six sacks in there for them to find, and to take away with them." He faced the outlaws. "Do you know what pyrites are?"

66

They didn't. Doria took a chance, though, and said, "A tribe of In'ians?"

"No. It looks like gold but it is not gold."

Spencer's face brightened. "Sure. I heard fellers talk about that stuff up in Montana. They called it fool's gold."

Sotelo smiled. "*Si*. Fool's gold."

"And that's what you left in the tunnel?"

"Yes. And I will hide for two weeks. Maybe longer, until Alvarado is gone."

"Yeah? And what about the deputy sheriff? He'll still be around and he's interested in your gold too."

Calvo's answer was short. "I know the deputy. I know him very well. For two sacks of gold he will forget there were two outlaws and that I helped them."

Doria thought it was a poor plan and said so, but Sotelo would not be budged. "I know where there is another old tunnel. Not a very good one because the *gauchupínes* found no gold over there, and abandoned it. I have water there and food, and no one can find me . . . *Señores*—the sun is coming. I am thankful. You are good friends and good men. I will remember that. But now you had better head east to the arroyo and ride for the border—and may God go with you."

The Mexican touched his floppy hatbrim, turned with the hawg-leg six-gun dangling at his side, and purposefully strode away.

They watched him disappear into the thorny under-brush, sat a few moments longer, then Doria shook his head and turned eastward without a word.

Spencer muttered to himself as he followed along. Sotelo had been right about daylight, it was beginning even now to softly brighten the hushed and still desert world.

They found the arroyo eventually. It had probably been carved from the plain several hundreds of years earlier by some horrific flash-flood. It was easily a hundred feet wide and at its most shallow place was not less than forty feet deep. There were trees down there, underbrush, and lush grass which seemed to derive nourishment from the very bottom of the arroyo where the ground was slightly spongy, as though perhaps there was water not far below the surface.

It was also full of wildlife. They even startled some deer, creatures which normally did not live on the desert at all, even in the springtime. There were coyote burrows and the smaller, better hidden dens of little desert foxes.

Birds bitterly scolded the horsemen as they worked their way along southward. Some of the birds even followed after them amid treetops to be certain the interlopers actually continued on out of their domain.

The sunlight did not reach down here but it flooded all the upper desert, and by the time there was full-day heat, the coolness of the arroyo was a distinct blessing.

They rode for three hours without halting, then swung off beside a clear-water pool, loosened cinchas, slipped bridles so the horses could eat, then Doria found a place where he could scale upward and stand on the rim looking around.

If there was any pursuit it was nowhere in sight. Doria slid back down to the pool where Spencer was stripped to the waist sluicing off. "Empty land up there," he reported. Spencer flung off water and stood up refreshed. "We got to get out of here and head back where we hid the saddlebags."

Doria was willing. "Tonight," he said, and flung down his hat to also strip to the waist and wash at the pool. "But right now I'm going to sleep for a while."

"Sleep! Those bastards can pick up our tracks and follow them down to this spot."

"Not for a couple of hours I hope," stated Jim Doria, beginning to wash. "This damned water is colder'n a lawman's heart."

Spencer turned without further argument and also scaled the slope. But he did not return, he scouted for a short distance, then found some shade beneath a big bush and sat down to keep watch. He might have also dozed off but the bush he had decided to sit in the shade of was also the cool residence of a very large old rattlesnake. The reptile responded to the sounds overhead by poking just his head out at first, until he saw the form of the biped which had been making that noise while he got comfortably settled, then the snake slithered out of his hole to make known that this was his turf. He got fairly close to Spencer, who was sitting with his hat back rolling a smoke then the rattler sinuously coiled, raised his head in front and from the middle of the coil raised his tail—and fiercely rattled.

Spencer did not look around. He sprang up and

away so swiftly he spilled his tobacco and lost his hat. From a hundred feet distant he turned, gun in hand. The old snake was still fiercely rattling but his head was now lower to the ground, lidless yellowish eyes fixed upon the white-faced man who was far out of reach.

Spencer's finger curled around the trigger as his Colt moved unerringly to bear. But he did not fire. Instead he said, "You scaly son of a bitch I'd give five thousand dollars right this minute to be able to pull this trigger."

The snake's noise diminished, then stopped completely although the reptile did not relinquish his coil nor raise his head from its striking position.

Spencer eyed his hat, saw the spilled tobacco and the sack from which it had fallen, slowly straightened up to holster his Colt, and turned to look elsewhere, under other bushes in case there was a den of rattlers close by. Then he dried his palms on a soiled blue bandanna, mopped his ashen face and turned limp all over. He had seen rattlesnakes before. This one seemed to be about five or six feet long, although it was difficult to make an accurate estimate as long as the creature was coiled, and it was as thick as a man's wrist. This *size* snake he was sure he had never before encountered. He was sure that if such an encounter had taken place he would have remembered it because Paul Spencer loathed all snakes. He particularly loathed rattlesnakes.

It required a full hour for that old snake to unwind

and return to his den, and if the day had not been hot he might have lingered longer.

Spencer retrieved his hat, considered filling the snake's hole, did not do it because he did not want to get that close, and picked up enough spilled tobacco to make one smoke, then he went out into the hot sunlight to stand smoking it while he alternately looked for riders, and additional rattlesnakes.

Doria was still asleep on the grass near the little pool when Spencer finally returned and awakened him to relate his adventure. Doria sat up, yawned, looked around where the horses were also dozing, full of grass now, and said, "Snakes won't bother you, Paul. That snake was just letting you know you were trespassing . . . Let's get a-horseback."

"Won't bother you! You didn't see the size of that son of a bitch. Thick as a man's arm and longer'n any snake's got a right to be. And mean-looking. Won't bother you! Hell of a lot you know about snakes . . . I'm never comin' back down through here again if it means I got to go back to punching cows for a living!"

They had to continue southward almost to the end of the arroyo to find a place where the horses could scramble up and out. By then Paul was over his fright and shock. Doria had done little to mitigate it; as they had been riding along he recounted instances he had heard of where rattlers had crawled into men's bedrolls for warmth at night, and other cases where rattlers had been inside men's boots when they had arisen in the morning to dress.

They sat motionless upon the desert for a long while, but there was no sign of pursuit. They did not doubt for a moment but that it was back there, somewhere, probably down in the arroyo, but even after wasting an hour it did not seem to be close, so they struck out on an angling course toward the distant place where they had hidden their outfits and their money.

The heat was noticeable. More noticeable than it had been in several days, and that filmy overcast which had been in evidence the day before was gone, so there was nothing to interfere with sunlight. Also, the south desert was paved with a variety of sandy grit which had as a major component infinitesimal flakes of mica, and each tiny flake reflected sunlight upward.

Spencer cursed the land. Doria paid no attention. They had sweated out most of the water they had consumed in the arroyo by the time they were in the vicinity of their cache, but there had been that big old stone trough under the trees at the cache-site and they pinned their hopes upon that.

Except that the shaggy old trees were visible high above the scaly underbrush, they might have had some difficulty locating their cache again. Even the best-oriented rangemen got lost on the south desert. There were scattered bones to prove it.

Doria was chary as they came closer. He led them on a big sashay on all sides looking for fresh horse-marks. He told Paul he was not convinced those rangeriders who had retrieved the stolen grays might not have had time to decide—from saddle marks, for example—that the grays had not wandered down this far by themselves.

Finally, they tethered the horses and crept ahead on foot.

Apparently, it was a futile precaution. Not only was there no indication that horsemen had been around, but there was birdsong from the treetops, and a pair of waddling armadillos were rummaging the ground, probably on the trail of the salt-sweat scent of leather.

Doria walked openly to the small green place, stood with hands on hips looking, then picked up a stone and flipped it into the trough. The armored creatures raised elongated faces with distinctive ears, then waddled away.

Paul walked forth and stared. "What in the hell are those things?"

Doria was heading for the place where they had hidden the saddlebags as he answered. "Sort of big, armored hedgehog. When something scares 'em they roll into a ball with their shell covering all their soft parts. The Mexicans call them armadillos."

"Are they poisonous too?"

"No." Doria ignored the creatures but Spencer kept his eye on them.

"I never saw such a worthless country," he exclaimed. "Even the animals down here are different. That blasted spider—big as my fist. And that snake— long as a lass-rope." He eyed the waddling armadillos. "What the hell good is something like that? Do folks eat 'em?"

Doria sank to both knees to begin gouging dirt without bothering to answer. They were now on the last leg of their journey and they had been a very long time getting this far.

Just a few more miles, with the saddlebags full of money . . . He felt leather, gripping it and pulled the saddlebags free. Spencer stopped talking.

Doria mopped at sweat, flung the bags to his partner and stood up to finish mopping off the perspiration. From a very great distance they heard a horse whinny.

It acted like a triggered mechanism. They hastened back to the horses, snugged up and climbed aboard, then turned due southward.

The sun was slightly off-center, the heat was a blight, but their stolen horses were conditioned-tough and in the thick, flourishing stands of underbrush no one would be able to find two horsemen unless they abruptly came upon them, not even trackers, because the two horsemen would not remain still for more than a few moments at a time.

Spencer borrowed tobacco from Doria, who had in turn appropriated it from those men back at Sotelo's house. As he lit up he said, "They better be able to speak *gringo* down across the border, Jim."

That had never worried Doria. It did not worry him now. He patted the bulging saddlebags. "This here green stuff talks a language everyone understands."

8
WELCOME!

Visible in a small brushed-off place where Doria halted to point was a cairn of white-painted stones. They had been many days reaching this point. Beyond the border-marker lay Mexico.

They continued on through a countryside which seemed no different from the territory they had just left, but after several miles they began to encounter rude little faggot corrals and equally as rude mud houses, commonly without windows and with doorways but no doors.

Occasionally a mahogany-colored child, or perhaps a coarse-featured man would step forth to silently watch them ride past. No one waved a greeting and it was obvious no one was pleased to see a pair of *gringos* coming south across the border. No one had to explain to Spencer that the few people they saw knew exactly what the pair of *Norteamericanos* were; this was outlaw country.

It was also hot country with only an occasional pair of meandering ruts to serve as roads. North of the border there was obvious hardship and evidence of spotty destitution but below the border destitution and hardship predominated. Even when they finally saw a town, where the land sloped a little toward a turgid, muddy stream of water, there still were no indications of even moderate prosperity, and the people they encountered on the outskirts of the town furtively looked up, then turned away, as they chose not to see two more *gringo pistoleros.*

The town was called Santa Maria and its liverybarn was housed in a low, rambling adobe structure which was so cool inside that when Spencer and Doria rode in and swung off, they felt almost chilled after hours of springtime desert.

The hostlers were Mexicans, ragged, smiling, servile men, but when the liveryman came out of his little cluttered office he was a round-faced, beefy *gringo* with a paunch and a pair of small, unblinking eyes which reminded Paul Spencer of that rattlesnake he had met earlier.

The liveryman smiled, motioned for their horses to be led away and cared for, then he studied Spencer and Doria, the latter with a pair of saddlebags across his shoulder and the tie-down hanging loose from his six-gun.

"Welcome to Santa Maria, gents," the thick-bodied liveryman said, making his knowledgeable assessment of two more soiled, stained, hard-eyed strangers. "We got a rooming-house up the road on the other side, and a saloon beside it, and we got a 'Merican café opposite the saloon . . . an' we got our own law here—it's Mex but we own it . . . an' we got a special service we offer newcomers for two dollars a day . . . Mex spies who make out like they're herdin' goats up close to the border to watch an' see if anyone will cross the line after you."

Doria's eyes brightened. "All the conveniences of home."

The heavy-set liveryman laughed. "For a price, gents. We got whatever you want, here in Santa Maria, for a price. And we got something else—Mex *rurales.* They are Mex constabulary troops. They got the right in Mexico to try you for a crime in the roadway, and shoot you if they find you guilty. They're sort of like soldiers, only a hell of a lot worse."

Doria was beginning to understand. "But for a price they leave folks alone."

The liveryman briskly nodded. "You sure figure things out fast, Mister Jones. And your partner there, Mister Smith." The wide grin reappeared. "Don't worry, you're plenty safe here. Enjoy yourself—but gents, no fighting. No shootin' or troublemaking. That's our rule here. Stay as long as you like just don't make trouble." The liveryman paused, then said, "My name is Jones too. Ain't that a coincidence? And you'll be surprised how many other fellers with names like Jones and Smith and Johnson and Jackson there are in Santa Maria." He winked. "Get settled in, gents, then set back and enjoy life." He walked away.

Spencer waited, then said, "Yeah; enjoy yourself-gents—as long as you can afford it."

They walked out into the treeless, dusty roadway and looked at the main thoroughfare of Santa Maria. Doria said, "Ugly town, Mister Smith."

There were Mexicans and little two-wheeled *caretas,* a few native horsemen and a sprinkling of other *gringos* using the dusty wide roadway. There were men of both races loafing under storefront *ramadas,* a few Mexican women, and dogs as well as filthy children playing in the dirt at roadside. Spencer and Doria were covertly studied as they strode up in the direction of the rooming-house, and up there they encountered a smiling thin youth of perhaps fifteen, who offered to haul water to the bath-house for them—for a dollar, an exorbitant price but after listening to the liveryman they were not too surprised, so they paid him, then went inside to get two rooms.

The man who operated the old adobe barracks which was now Santa Maria's rooming-house was a very thin, big-eyed, thin-lipped Texan with an ashen complexion and a racking cough. He never smiled and spoke only as much as he had to. He did not ask their names nor require their signatures in a register, he simply held out a thin hand for five dollars each for rooms, pointed to the back of the house and told them to take any pair of rooms which were not occupied, then walked away with their money.

Spencer scowled.

Later, at the bath-house with the grinning youth breathing hard from his exertions, they learned that only the day before the *rurales* had ridden away, and now everyone was able to breathe easily again. Doria considered the boy. He was their only acquaintance thus far who was open and friendly. Doria asked about other residents of the rooming-house and the youth rolled large, liquid dark eyes. In terrible English he said there were only six or eight other men staying there now, but last month there had been many more and they came and went, sometimes only remaining a day or two, and often they departed in the night without anyone knowing they were gone until the following morning.

Doria and Spencer returned to their adjoining rooms to rest, something they required more than they thought, and not until late at night did they meet again, out front on the rambling, decrepit veranda where several other residents of the rooming-house were sitting silently smoking and watching the southward roadway.

No one spoke, no one nodded. As Spencer and Doria headed for the saloon, the one brightly lighted place the full length of Santa Maria's roadway, Paul said, "This place reminds me of a graveyard where all the corpses are dressed and sitting up."

But the saloon was noisy. Not as noisy as some saloons but certainly different from the furtive, wary people outside who, especially in full daylight acted as though they belonged in darkness and wanted to be there.

They met the saloonman, his predatory grin fixed in place as he leaned at the bar and exchanged remarks with some of the other drinkers, but mostly with the barman, a graying, rawboned large man with two knife scars, both on the same, left, side of his hawk-like face.

The saloonman listened briefly to what the liveryman had to say while eyeing Spencer and Doria, then came along to swipe the bar where they stopped, and to cock a hard eye. "Drinks, gents?"

They ordered a bottle and two glasses, took them to a dingy, distant table and sat, backs to the wall, watching other patrons.

There were games at each of the card tables, and a raucous crowd at the crap table. There were also three unsmiling young men with shotguns in their laps seated on tilted-back chairs at different places throughout the room.

Doria tossed off a jolt of popskull and said, "The other time I was in Mexico it was west of here, and the town was different."

Spencer leaned to refill their glasses. "Any town would be different," he suggested, and wondered out loud how long outlaws had to remain in a place like Santa Maria before they felt safe to leave.

Doria's guess was sound enough. "Until someone commits a bigger crime where they committed theirs, then folks up in Rosario will forget about us in favor of someone else."

Spencer sipped his whisky. "That might be forever. Rosario likely won't have ten thousand dollars in its damned bank again for a hundred years." He sipped, watched, then also said, "Six months here would *be* a hundred years."

The liveryman came over, pulled out a chair and eased his bulk down with caution, smiling as he set his beer glass on the table. "You'll get used to it," he said "I see that same look on the faces of two-thirds of the lads who make it down here." He emitted a deep chuckle. "It's better'n the look on the faces of the fellers who get caught before they get down here."

He reached for his beer, drank, wiped his lips with a soiled sleeve and gestured. "It's all here, lads, and if you don't see it all you got to do ask and it'll show up."

Two cold-faced men entered, each with a tied-down Colt on the right side and a sawed-off scattergun in his left hand. A few men nodded to the pair and got curt nods back. The liveryman said, "Our law. Works best if we got two at a time. An' they got backups. Four other fellers who get paid in Yankee dollars for helpin' make things peaceable here. That tallest feller—the one with the notched ear—that's Texas Jack Evans. They say he's killed men from California to Sinaloa, to Chihuahua and back again."

Spencer leaned and gazed at the liveryman. "Who's the other one?"

"Feller who used to ride for Carter Alvarado. Feller named Steve something-or-other. I forget the rest of it. Steve's good enough anyway. You fellers ever hear of Carter Alvarado?"

They lied without opening their mouths. They both shook their heads and the liveryman leaned to get comfortable. "Best manhunter in the whole southwest. He gives marshals and sheriffs a piece of every reward bounty they set him on the trail of. He's got the slickest business around. Hires fellers to ride with him, pays 'em better'n rangemen and furnishes 'em with the best horses he can get hold of. Alvarado's never yet lost out. At least, if he ever did, no one knows about it. Once he's on their trail there's no place for them to go but straight up. He's half Yank, half Mex, and half devil . . . an' he owns a slice of Santa Maria."

The pair of lawmen made their round of the saloon then walked out. The barman jerked his head and the liveryman hoisted up to his feet to go over there.

Spencer said, "Well, that sure sounds great. We got the one son of a bitch on our trail who don't stop at the border—and we rode our dumb tails off to get down into Mexico where we'd be safe. Now what?"

Doria reached to refill his little shot-glass. "Leave I guess," he said, and tasted the liquor. "It's not like Alvarado is just after a reward. We stole two of his horses and tied up three of his riders . . . This isn't bad whisky, is it?"

Spencer considered the glass in his hand as though he did not realize how it had got there. "No, it's not bad at all," he confirmed. "For a man's last drink."

Doria watched two worn, dusty, lean men enter from the cool night and head for the bar as they struck dust from their trousers. "Like the kid said, Paul—they come and they go. Those two just came in."

The liveryman threw a casual wave and his smile in the direction of Spencer and Doria then went back out into the darkness.

Two poker players arose to stretch and yawn and cash in before heading for the bar. Those two newcomers saw empty chairs and headed for them. The other gamblers made them welcome and chips were stacked in red and blue and white stacks. Both the newcomers lit cigarettes, shoved back their hats, nursed their bottle and glasses, and fished around to pay for the chips.

Spencer was watching a pair of men rolling dice at the bar for drinks when Doria's hand lightly fell upon his arm and bore down, hard.

Spencer turned back. Those two newcomers at the poker table were paying for their chips from soiled little tobacco sacks which contained nuggets of pure gold.

None of the other players were too interested, but they called to the barman to fetch a scales before play commenced.

Doria had another half-jolt, sat back watching and saying nothing. Paul Spencer did the same for a while, until the poker session was in progress, then he sighed and put aside his glass.

"That damned old fool. Him and his cave where they'd never find him. I'll give you odds this time they didn't just tie him up and kick him a little. This time they got his gold and cut his throat."

Doria made and lit a smoke, still maintaining his silence. The poker game was in full swing. The newcomers were good at it; they won about as many pots as they lost, but the odds were against them winning too often because there were four other players at the table.

Jim finished his smoke and leaned to arise. "We better pay the gent for the bottle," he said, arising, heading for the bar and placing a greenback beside the bottle. The barman nodded matter-of-factly, removed the bottle and went away with the greenback. In Santa Maria, they gave no change.

Spencer got red but Doria nudged him and led the way outside where the night was cool and brilliant with more stars across the desert heavens than a man could have counted in a lifetime.

There were few people abroad outside the saloon. Doria strolled away from the door, nodded to a pair of shotgun-armed men who walked past, and when Spencer got over there he said, "Alvarado owns part of Santa Maria and he wants us for makin' him look bad up at Soledad—not to mention at Rosario . . . If those two we just saw with the tobacco sacks of the old man's gold are Alvarado's riders, then sure as hell the rest of the crew—and Alvarado—are right here in town . . . How good a chance do you expect we got of getting out of here before that fat liveryman tells Alvarado a couple of strangers rode in today—and shows him those horses we rode in on?"

Spencer listened, then glanced in the direction of the rooming-house. "Where did you hide the ten thousand dollars?"

Doria also looked up there. Four men were coming out into the gloom of the empty veranda. They had that emaciated-looking proprietor with them.

Doria said, "Where they didn't find it, this time. Let's get it, steal another couple of horses and get the hell out of here!"

9
A LONG NIGHT

They headed for the rooming-house, but not by a direct route, and the lanky man sitting in comfort smoking on the veranda, watching the roadway, was no one they had seen on the porch earlier in the day. Also, he was travel-stained.

It could have been a simple coincidence. It probably was one, but Doria and Spencer had learned in their trade that counting on coincidences could get someone killed, so they went around behind the room-house to confer—and encountered that ragged, smiling Mexican youth back there. He was hauling more water for someone's visit to the bath-house.

The boy put down his buckets, looked around, then spoke without smiling. "They are es-lookin' for you," he said. "There is one out front and one inside in the dark where he can see your rooms."

The youth held out a hand. This time it was Paul Spencer who peeled off a note and placed it upon the outstretched palm. "No way to get into the rooms?" he said, and the youth vigorously shook his head while pocketing the money. "No, *Señor*. I know those men. They ride with Alvarado."

Spencer turned. Jim Doria smiled at the youth, who

85

picked up his buckets and staggered on. Doria watched the youth enter the bath-house to dump his buckets. Spencer said, "We got to get into the rooms."

Doria cocked an eyebrow. "Why?"

"Why! For the ten thousand dollars, that's why?"

Doria smiled a little. "It's not in there, Paul." He pointed as the Mexican youth emerged carrying empty buckets. Spencer stared, said nothing until the grinning youth had trudged past on his way to the pump again, then Spencer said, *"There?"*

Doria led the way. He had cached his saddlebags beneath the rear of the bath-house where some digging varmint had made a large hole, then he had kicked dirt in the hole. Spencer stood and watched as Doria retrieved the saddlebags, then Spencer smiled with heartfelt relief. But as they turned away in the darkness, he began muttering about having to abandon his ivory-handled razor, his change of clothing, and a couple of wanted dodgers with good likenesses of him on them.

They went cautiously over behind Santa Maria on the west side among some adobe hovels which were dark, and which showed no signs of any kind of life, not even chickens nor dogs, two things which were almost always found in Mexican villages, and had a quiet smoke while they discussed their next move.

Clearly, Alvarado's watchmen were also down at the liverybarn. Clearly too, it was a matter of time before the dragnet would tighten. If, as the liveryman had said, Carter Alvarado owned a piece of Santa Maria, he would not have to rely upon his riders only. He would be able to also rely upon those shotgun-lawmen the liveryman had mentioned, and perhaps others as well.

Spencer said, "The first two sound-lookin' saddle-horses we see, Jim," and Doria dropped his smoke as he nodded.

Spencer smiled, for some reason, as he turned to head back into the darkness of town from the west side. His step was lighter too. It was one of the inherent quirks of Paul Spencer's nature that he functioned best under stress and in danger. Even his normally skeptical, distrustful disposition improved.

Santa Maria did not have very many saddled horses along its roadway, not even over in front of the saloon. Mostly, its fugitive-inhabitants did not ride out very much. Many of them never left town at all. They were safe within Santa Maria's environs. Beyond, there was always the chance of being ambushed and sold back over the line to U.S. lawmen.

But Doria and Spencer only required two horses. There were certainly many more than that in sight as the pair of robbers emerged from between two dark storefronts to stand looking up and down the roadway.

There were also a number of men quietly loafing in the moonlight, several up in front of the saloon, several more down in front of a general store. Although it was late now, the night not as warm as it had been earlier, it was still pleasant out. The chill would not arrive for several hours yet, shortly before dawn.

Doria was disappointed. "If those fellers would go inside the saloon. . . ."

Spencer jutted his chin. "There's that long-legged feller who was sitting on the porch at the rooming-house, and he's walkin' toward the saloon like he's got something on his mind." Spencer's eyes narrowed as he watched. "You don't reckon that kid sold us out do you?"

Doria only fleetingly considered this possibility. He said, "The liverybarn, Paul, that all we got left."

They went back out behind town again and walked southward. Not a word was said until they got close to the mud back-wall down there and looked in. The fat liveryman was not smiling for a change, in his conversation with a coppery-colored, slightly beefy man who wore an ivory-handled six-gun tied down. Slightly to the rear of the man with the ivory-handle were two other men, younger and taller, looking faded and menacing even though that lamplight was not really very good up in the center of the runway.

Doria whispered. "Care to make a hundred-dollar bet?"

Spencer was studying those four men when he replied. "On what?"

"That son of a bitch with the fancy pistol is Alvarado."

Spencer's brows pulled inward and slightly downward. "You ever see him before?"

"Nope. But if that's not him my hunch is plumb wrong, and usually I got good hunches."

"Hunches hell," murmured Spencer, pulling gently back. "We need horses, not hunches."

88

They waited ten minutes before the three strangers walked out front with the liveryman trailing, still talking, then they got inside the barn.

The building seemed empty of other people but to be sure they prowled among the stalls, then they heard the liveryman returning and stepped into a dark stall to wait and watch.

There were at least a dozen stalled horses in the old building making sounds, and eating. The liveryman came down as far as the entrance to his little office, then paused to look around, and curse under his breath. Then he entered the office.

Doria had already decided on a big rawboned sorrel horse and as he stepped forth he pointed toward a seal brown gelding. Spencer eyed the horse, then eyed the place where the harness and saddlery was kept. Doria stepped past and went over to take a position to one side of the office. Spencer got the seal-brown horse and led him forth, then Doria pointed to the sorrel horse and this time as Spencer walked to the stall to open the door and lead the horse out, the liveryman's chair squeaked as he heaved up to his feet, attracted by the sounds in the runway. Spencer did not even look around as he went after two saddles, blankets and bridles. He was hauling the outfits back where the horses were standing when the liveryman stepped out and halted to stare.

He must have recognized Spencer because his mouth dropped open. For five seconds, with Paul ignoring him, the liveryman simply stood staring, then he said, "Hey; that's not your horse."

Spencer looked across the horse's back. "What did you say, you got to come a little closer I don't hear too good."

The fat man took several steps closer. "I said—that ain't your horse!"

Spencer straightened up. "Really?" he stepped back to look at the animal. "It's so darned dark in here. . . ."

The liveryman walked still closer, anger showing in the way he stood with both hands on his hips. "Mister, I told you—we got plenty of our own law here in Santa Maria. You better put that horse back in his stall."

Spencer gazed at the fat man, then settled the blanket and leaned to hoist the saddle. "That feller who was in here a few minutes ago—the feller with the fancy gun-handle—was that Carter Alvarado?"

"It was," exclaimed the angry liveryman.

"And," stated Paul Spencer, settling the saddle and leading to reach for the cincha, "you told him about my partner and me?"

The liveryman did not answer. It must have suddenly occurred to him that there was probably another one of them somewhere around. He twisted to look back.

Doria was standing in the gloom of the wall, both thumbs hooked in his shellbelt, his face expressionless as he looked at the liveryman.

Now, finally, the liveryman understood exactly what was happening. "I ain't armed," he exclaimed.

Spencer finished with the saddle and stepped ahead to fit the bridle. "Don't matter," he replied to the liveryman. "What did Alvarado want in here—if you lie you'll wish you hadn't."

"He was lookin' for you two. And he'll find you. He was willin' to pay a hundred dollars to anyone who knew where you fellers was."

"What did you tell him?"

"What could I tell him? That I ain't seen either of you since last night in the saloon an' before that not since yesterday morning."

Spencer smiled. "Master Jones—or was it Johnson—you're a right truthful man. That might even keep you alive a little longer."

Spencer went after the second horse, the rawboned big sorrel, and led him forth to also be rigged out. The liveryman watched without opening his mouth until Spencer was again hoisting a saddle, then he said, "You take those two horses, fellers, and you're not just goin' to have Alvarado after you—half the fellers here in town'll be after you. That's one thing we got rules against—horse-stealing."

Spencer went right on working. "And where did the feller who rode this horse down here steal him?"

The liveryman turned for another glance backwards. "You fellers ain't going to make it," he told Doria. "Alvarado's hot as hell about you boys."

Doria still said nothing, but he walked ahead to take the reins Spencer held out to him, and as he turned the horse a couple of times before mounting, he ended up close to the fat man. "Everything down here is for sale for a price, Mister Johnson. That's what you told us."

In anticipation of what Doria had in mind the fat man began to emphatically shake his head. "I can't do it. Not with Alvarado. I can't lie to him. Anyway, those two horses you got—that big sorrel belongs to Alvarado and the seal-brown belongs to his right-hand-man, John Hunt."

Doria said, "That's too bad, Mister Johnson," and swung so hard and fast the fat man could not get untracked to avoid the blow. He went down in a heap. Doria wiggled his gloved fist then turned to step up across leather.

They rode out the back of the barn and did not go up through the dark west side of town but kept on riding due west for an hour before finally turning northward again.

Spencer said, "You'd ought to have busted him down with your gunbarrel. Using your right fist will make the knuckles swell."

Doria stood in his stirrups to look back, then settled down again. "I thought someone like Alvarado would ride a racy-lookin' thoroughbred."

They made good time. Two hours later they knew why Carter Alvarado rode the rawboned big sorrel horse. He was tireless. Where they crossed the border riding north, a hint of first-light shone from one of those piles of white-painted stones and Spencer said, "You know, Jim, seems to me you got to keep on earnin' your wages in this danged business over and over. I wonder, if we ever figured it out by the hour, just how much we make?"

"Not too darned much for a fact," replied Doria. "Seems to me it's gettin' harder every day to keep it . . . You expect Alvarado would hand it over to the law up in Rosario if he got it away from us?"

"Sure. He'd hand it back like the devil would buy icewater." Spencer considered the seal-brown horse he was riding. "Good animal. Better'n those other two we stole from Alvarado. It just occurred to me— Alvarado's helpin' us quite a bit."

"Remind me to thank him when we meet."

"If you get the time . . . Where do we head from here?"

"Soledad."

Spencer turned looking surprised, then he looked annoyed, and finally he looked ahead through the chilly graying pre-dawn. "Maybe we should have waylaid those two at the saloon and taken the sacks of gold back with us.

Doria had no comment to offer about that, but a mile or so farther along he gestured for Spencer to halt. They sat a long while listening before Doria said, "Hell, I thought Alvarado was quicker than that. You hear anything?"

"No, and I'm not even a little bit disappointed."

They kept riding and when dawn finally arrived they halted upon a low landswell which had no brush upon it, for a change, and looked back. This time they saw the dust. Spencer watched for a while then said, "We better head out and around, find us a road to mingle our tracks with."

They went westward for more than a mile without finding any road. There was none down through this part of the border country. But eventually they came across a place where mustangs had crossed through recently, but that did not help much because their mounts were shod and the wild horses hadn't been, although it would slow down the pursuit long enough for their hunters to pick shod marks from unshod ones in the gritty soil.

They also sought rock outcrops, but even when they found them none of the rock ledges was very large, so in the end as they got steadily closer to Soledad they decided they would be unable to elude the pursuit and concentrated instead upon keeping ahead of it.

Alvarado's crew had slackened off from their initial rage-motivated pursuit and were now making steady walking progress, which was actually the best way for manhunters to catch their prey.

But Doria and Spencer had been through this before and they were still alive and free so they had to be fairly good at it too. Where they failed to preserve was when they were in sight of Soledad, and halted again, this time to sit a while, roll smokes and discuss their next move.

Doria thought they should return to Sotelo's abode but Spencer was of the opinion that Alvarado had probably left the old faggot-gatherer's body out near his mine somewhere for the buzzards and coyotes to glean. Nevertheless he agreed that since they were this close they might as well go over around to Mex-town, which is what they did.

They left their stolen horses and covered the remaining distance on foot. Several people were abroad in the cool, pleasant morning. One was a fat woman, very dark with a flat Indian-face, whose black eyes watched their progress as she draped her wash from a rope clothesline. Two others were men as old as Calvo Sotelo hoeing in a weedy garden patch out behind the adobe church. They used any excuse to lean upon their hoes, and this excuse seemed more valid than most.

When Doria and Spencer reached the Sotelo adobe and peeked in a handsome, buxom woman with eyes and hair as black as midnight, glanced up—and froze with a hand to her full lips. She did not utter a sound but she looked as though she might so Doria said, "Friends, lady. We're friends of the old gent who lives here." He stepped inside in the cool gloom. The woman acted as though she either had not heard or did not believe.

Spencer moved around her and stopped stone-still looking at the still form on the wall-bed. He said, very softly, "Those lousy bastards."

Calvo Sotelo was bloody and inert on the bed. Doria went over to also look. "Dead?" he murmured.

Spencer went closer and leaned to make certain. "Darn near it," he replied. "How did he ever get back here in his shape?"

The woman finally spoke. "The burro brought him,

Señores." She moved over beside them, also looking down. "He is my father. They thought they had killed him. He has been shot and beaten." Her voice caught, she put both hands to her mouth again.

Doria turned toward the little rickety table where there was an earthen basin with pinkish water in it, tossed down his hat and ran bent fingers through his curly dark hair. "They got his gold," he told the woman without looking around. "We saw a couple of them using it in a poker game down in Santa Maria." He turned. "Your paw did a darned dumb thing, *Señora*. He tried to outsmart Alvarado."

The woman's eyes widened on Doria. "You. . . . *Señor*. . . .?

"Me? Alvarado? Not by a darned sight, lady. But he's on his way back here."

The woman groaned.

Paul Spencer turned from the old man with granite eyes. "I can understand a feller chasin' *us*. I can't understand someone doing *that* to an unarmed old man. You know what I think, Jim?"

Doria nodded his head. "Yeah. But we better not be caught in here when we try it. This time, the son of a bitch is likely to have more than just his five scalp-hunters along." Doria faced the woman. "Lady, does your paw have friends around here? If he does, you might pass the word that Alvarado's returning, and right now your paw needs eight or ten men with guns to be here in case Alvarado comes back to finish him off . . . And lady, you know the deputy here in Soledad?"

96

"*Si.* Yes, I know him."

"Where does he hang out this time of the morning?"

"Maybe at his jailhouse, *Señores.* Maybe at the card-room in the back of the saloon . . . *Señores?* "

"Just look after your paw," said Doria, "forget we were here, but if the old gent comes round, tell him those two fellers he helped a few days back are goin' to be around town for a spell, and for him not to worry too much."

After they had walked back out into the morning coolness Spencer scowled. "What do you mean, the old gent shouldn't worry too much? Anybody Alvarado is after had better worry."

Doria said, "Us mainly. I didn't want the old man to be worrying, nor the woman. She sure is pretty isn't she?"

Spencer rolled his eyes. "Partner, we're standing with one foot in our graves and the other foot on a banana peel, and you want to talk about pretty women!"

10
THE MORNING SUN

They thought they might have as much as an hour. Perhaps a little less but certainly more than a half-hour before Alvarado reached Soledad, so they hid their stolen horses in that same empty shed they had hidden the other stolen horses in when they had been up here before, then they went briskly to the jailhouse—from out back.

Someone upon the opposite side of town was shaping a hot shoe on an anvil. The sound was rhythmic and musical. There were assorted other sounds as Soledad came progressively to life in the early morning. Spencer banged on the steel-reinforced rear door of the jailhouse and Doria stood back and to one side.

They had a long wait before a stocky man with a pulled-down thin mouth and unpleasant cold eyes swung the door inward. He was large and thick and he was holding a cup of coffee in his left hand.

Spencer stepped up and without a word pushed the large man backwards, hard, then he stepped inside and a moment later Doria also walked into the jailhouse. The deputy swore when hot coffee spilled on him and turned with a snarl. Doria's arm did not seem to move at all, but as his hand steadied up there was a gun in it.

The big deputy looked from the gun to Doria's expressionless face, eyes widening a little at a time. "By gawd," he exclaimed. "I know you. I know who you are!"

Spencer smiled. "Go on back into the front office . . . Is that fresh coffee?"

The three of them went through the storeroom to the office, which was a small, stale-smelling room with barred windows toward the roadway beyond. The deputy turned, set down his cup and straightened up. "You'll never make it," he stated.

Spencer was still smiling. "Then we'll take you with us. Where are the keys to the cells?"

The big man looked uncertain. When Doria holstered his Colt the big man eyed him carefully without speaking or moving.

Spencer's smile began to fade. "You son of a bitch, we don't have all day. The keys!"

Finally, the deputy fished in a shirt-pocket and tossed one large brass key to Spencer. The three of them went through another of those steel-reinforced oak doors into another small room which smelled bad. There were three cells. They disarmed the deputy and pushed him into the first one, locked the door and Spencer's smile returned.

"We'll be back to peel some hide off you, Deputy."

Doria stepped closer to the straps of steel. "Maybe we'd better peel some off right now," he said, and did not blink as the large lawman's face settled into a brutish, confident expression. "You think we can't do it, Deputy?"

The lawman's answer was a rumble. "Not without no gun you can't."

Doria studied the big, powerful man. "Maybe you're right. Maybe we'd have to knee-shoot you to make things a little more even. But mister, we can do it, one way or another . . . Why did you beat hell out of the old Mex?"

"What old Mex?"

Doria motioned toward the door. "Open it, Paul, I think we'd ought to bust him up a little."

Spencer made no move to unlock the door but he said, "Deputy, I told you—we don't have all day. Personally, I'd as leave pot-shoot you in that cage. You got five seconds to answer. Why did you help Alvarado beat hell out of the old Mex?"

The large man hesitated, studying them both, then arrived at his decision. "I never touched Sotelo. I went out to his mine with them but I never laid a hand on him."

"Who did?"

"Alvarado and two of his men."

"But you told them there was gold," said Doria, running a bluff that worked.

"All I knew was what a Mex who informs for me told me about Sotelo goin' up there and comin' back a lot. This other Mex spied on him. He said he was sure the old goat-herder had found a vein in that old Spanish mine. I told Alvarado. We went up there. . . ."

"And caught the old man?"

"No. We went to look at the shaft and see if he could find a cache. The old Mex was here in town."

"Did you find anything up there?"

"No. So we come back and went over to the Sotelo adobe."

"And beat the old man."

"Not me. I stood outside. *They* beat him."

"Who shot him?"

The deputy stared. "No one shot him."

"The hell they didn't. Someone shot him last night, and beat hell out of him again. He's at his shack now more dead than alive."

The deputy was clearly surprised. "The last I saw of

100

Carter Alvarado was when he said he was goin' down to Santa Maria after you fellers. That was yesterday in broad daylight."

"He didn't get down there until midnight last night," stated Doria. "It's not that far a ride. So—he went after the old Mex again, and this time he got it out of him and took his little sacks of gold."

"By gawd I didn't know a thing about that," exclaimed the deputy. "I'm tellin' you the plain truth. He never said anything about going back after the old goat-herder again. I didn't see him around town last night so I figured he'd gone south."

Doria said, "I kind of hope you're lying, mister. I want to get you out in the roadway of your own damned town in front of everybody, and call you . . . They'll bury you tomorrow night."

The lawman's look of confidence was not as solid as it had been earlier when Doria had wanted to go inside the cell with him. He had seen Doria's draw. He undoubtedly still felt convinced he could handle Doria with fists, but that had been an incredibly fast draw and as a south-desert lawman in an area where gunmen were commonplace, the deputy knew real gunmen when he saw them.

"You ask Sotelo if I laid a hand on him," he exclaimed.

"But if you'd found his gold when you were with Alvarado you'd have taken your share of it," Doria said, and turned his back. "Let's get out of here, Paul. This keeps smellin' worse by the minute."

As Doria turned up the little corridor Paul Spencer smiled at their locked-in lawman. "You so much as make a peep to let folks know you're locked in here, mister and you'll wish you hadn't."

Up in the little office Doria was helping himself to a cup of coffee from the little iron stove when his partner emerged from the cell-room, turned and closed the cell-room door.

"Is that fresh coffee?" Spencer asked.

Doria tasted it. "Yeah. Blacker'n original sin and ten times as strong though."

They stood a moment in thought, sipping their coffee. Spencer said, "He'd ought to ride in any time now. You want to get caught in here—in a lousy jail-house? They make me nervous and besides, this one don't smell very good."

Doria looked around. "You reckon that two-legged horse has got any food in here?"

Spencer looked pained. "I said—Alvarado's goin' to ride in here any minute now."

Doria finished the coffee and set the cup aside. "Paul, you're a worrier."

Spencer snorted. "Me, a worrier? Why in hell would I be worryin' with only Alvarado and a bunch of *pistoleros* slippin' into town wantin' to kill us?"

They left the jailhouse by the same back-alley doorway they had used to enter it. The sun was high, heat was building up, a bony-tailed big old slab-sided dog was out back rummaging in trash cans, and at sight of the two men, he whisked from sight beyond a tumble-down wooden shed northward and across the alley.

Doria said, "They're going to land at the liverybarn first. I'd like to know how many of them there are."

"What *I'd* like," said his partner, "would be ten or twelve fellers on our side for a change. Jim, we got to get out of this business."

"Yeah, I know. Buy a decent saloon in a decent town and set back and rest a lot . . . Let's go."

"Where?"

"You take the west side of the road and I'll take the east side, and get down near the liverybarn."

"Maybe there's twenty of them."

"Then we'll have to reload a couple of times."

Spencer said, "There was some shotguns in the rack in the jailhouse. That'd whittle down the odds a little."

"Not the width of the roadway it wouldn't," stared Doria. "And those darned things kick like an army mule . . . You want to stand here playin' like you're an army general or should we just split up and tackle the first ones we see—and try hardest for that copperhead with the ivory gun-handle?"

"Maybe more'n twenty of them, Jim."

"Can't find out but one way, Paul. And the first couple of jumps we'll be ahead of them because they won't expect us."

Spencer sighed. "But Saint Peter will," he said, and turned to follow Doria down the alley until they came to a trash-littered vacant site between two old adobe buildings. The heat was increasing and across the road a man without sleeves in his faded shirt, and arms like young oak trees strolled forth from the café wiping his lips with the back of one broad, scarred big hand.

The town was quiet. There were neither horsemen nor very many people on foot now, as the initial bustle of morning had faded along toward the hot time of midday. A Mexican driving a small burro turned up out of the east side of town and went plodding southward upon some private mission down across the desert.

Doria and Spencer stepped into the shade of a storefront and each man rolled a smoke, then they stood looking up and down the roadway. In the area of the liverybarn there was one sprawled dog in tree-shade and a man either dozing or asleep upon a stone bench near a stone trough.

Spencer shook his head. "They should have ridden in by now. If they were down there that dog wouldn't be lying there."

Doria was unconcerned. "Good. Maybe we got a few minutes to get something to eat at the café."

Spencer got that pained look again. "We won't have *that* much time."

Doria shrugged. "Let's go find out. I can be a lot meaner on a full stomach."

They crossed to the café. The town around them was as drowsy and quiet as it usually was this time of day, and later. There was no hint at all that trouble was in the making, or that a body of heavily-armed horsemen was approaching from the direction of the south border.

The caféman was a sweating, pulpy individual with scarcely any hair and a soft, pale look to him. After he had taken their orders and gone away, Spencer said, "He looks like a big fat slug from under a rock."

Doria killed his smoke underfoot and twisted on the bench to gaze out into the hushed and sun-bright roadway. "Maybe Alvarado changed his mind—for some reason."

"Maybe you're hopin' that harder than you'd ought to be. He'll be along. So far we've knocked out three of his men, stole four of his horses, including his own private horse, and made him look bad by not lettin' him catch up to us . . . He'll be along."

11
CONVERGING RIDERS

They finished two fair-sized meals, refused the oily coffee, paid up and went outside. Three Mexicans were upon the opposite side of the road from the saloon. Two more were loafing out front of a store down near the jailhouse. They were *vaqueros* by their looks and attire, youngish, lean, bronzed men, without equal in the southwest as cowboys.

Otherwise, except for several old men sitting in the shade out front of the general store, sopping up the same heat most other people were now avoiding, the roadway was empty and quiet.

Spencer lit a smoke. "What in hell's holding him up? We saw his dust and he wasn't this far behind us."

Paul kept watching the lower end of town. "I'd like for the son of a bitch to ride right up into town from down there, in plain sight, so we could get this over with."

"He's not that dumb," stated Doria, more relaxed where he was standing in shade. "He knows we're here and he knows we're not greenhorns. I got a hunch Carter Alvarado thinks like a snake and works like a wolf."

A thin, slightly stooped, crafty-faced Mexican emerged from between two buildings heading briskly for the jailhouse. Doria and Spencer watched him. "The informer," Doria murmured.

Spencer whipped upright. "If he goes in there he'll find the deputy locked up."

One of those loafing Mexicans across the road turned to casually intercept the crafty-faced man. They met directly in front of the jailhouse door and whatever was said did not take but a moment, then the crafty-faced man turned abruptly and walked away. The *vaquera* ambled back to his companion and they resumed their loafing stance.

Spencer scowled. "What was that about?"

Doria trickled smoke while eyeing the Mexicans. Then he turned to look northward where those other *vaqueros* were loafing opposite the saloon before he said, "Paul, I think maybe we got some reinforcements."

Spencer's gaze moved back and forth from one group of *vaqueros* to the other. He said nothing but his expression showed quick, hard interest.

A solitary rangerider entered town from the north riding at a walk. He was dusty and slumped as though he had come a long distance and was tired. He found a shady place to tie his horse then went stolidly in the direction of the saloon knocking off dust as he walked.

The sun did not seem to be moving, there was a thin veil of heat-haze far out, and although it was still springtime it was obviously getting along toward summer. Unless people knew no other existence or unless they had very good personal reasons for being on the south desert in summertime, they would begin drifting northward soon now. The heat was debilitating once full summer arrived, and while houses with three-feet-thick mud walls mitigated it, people could not remain indoors forever.

The cowboy disappeared beyond the front of the saloon and that old Mexican with the little burro who had gone plodding southward out of town earlier, now reappeared with a light load of faggots on his burro. He did not lead his burro as many Mexicans did, he herded it from behind using a stick to tap one side of its rump or the other side and the burro, having been broke like this, willingly obeyed each light tap.

This time, the faggot-gatherer did not turn off heading back into Mex-town, he shuffled through the dust up to the area near the jailhouse where those two lean *vaqueros* were leaning, said something to them and kept right on steering his burro with the stick. He passed Doria and Spencer with just one look, then went on his way.

Doria dropped his smoke and stamped it out. "My hunch," murmured, "is that there's something going on here."

Spencer, who had scarcely more than spared a glance at the old man with the burro, answered bleakly. "Yeah. We're standin' here like sittin' ducks—and Alvarado probably got into town from out back somewhere and right now is settin' us up like targets in a shootin' gallery."

Doria turned as a young Mexican boy of perhaps fifteen or sixteen came from between two buildings and turned toward them. As he walked past he shoved a piece of paper into Doria's hand without more than briefly glancing around, then he hurried on by and disappeared into the general store.

Doria and Spencer leaned to study the slip of paper. It conveyed a very brief message: 'There are four of them. They are coming two to one side of town, two on the other side.'

Spencer scratched, re-read the note then craned around for the youthful messenger who was no longer in sight. He puffed out his cheeks and gently expelled a breath of air. "You're right—for a change—we got reinforcements. Now—the question is—do Messicans run when trouble starts?"

"They don't," stated Doria, "if they got a reason not to. My guess is that the old gent's handsome daughter did like we told her to do—she rounded up some of his friends. I'd say that feller who stopped the informer is one of his friends and those other Mex cowboys are more of his friends." Doria looked else-where. "There could be some more of them around here."

He paused a moment before speaking again. That dusty, tired rangeman—or outlaw—emerged from the saloon stepping a little higher than when he entered, and went over to get his horse from the shady place. He piled aboard and reined southward down the empty roadway. When he came abreast of Doria and Spencer, Paul impulsively called softly to him.

"About twenty more miles, mister, and you're in Mexico."

The rider expressionlessly gazed at Paul, then at Jim, and finally his lips lifted in a little grudging smile and he nodded, then kept on riding.

"He'd ought to rest that horse and water him," Spencer said after the rider was gone.

Doria's interest in the rangeman was very brief. "Two on the west side of town and two on the east side. If we got friends on the east side, back in Mex-town, they might take care of the two coming from that direction." Doria frowned in thought for a moment before saying, "I figured he'd show up with a small army. At least the bunch he had when he was trying to ride us down."

Spencer's interest was more direct. "It only takes one bullet. He can have three fellers with him or thirty, it still only takes one bullet."

The Mexicans upon the opposite side of the roadway seemed disinterested and unconcerned, but when the three opposite the saloon saw a man step from between two buildings and pause to glance down the roadway, one of them spoke briefly with the other two then started toward the newcomer. Doria watched. Paul Spencer noticed nothing until the *vaquero* softly called to the stranger as the man turned in the direction of the saloon.

The stranger halted, studied the *vaquero,* then squared around to meet him, and when the *vaquero* was close enough to speak, the stranger stiffened slightly at something the *vaquero* said.

Doria and Spencer could not distinguish what had been said but they had no difficulty in making out the stranger's reaction. Then the Mexican halted a few feet from the stranger and gestured toward the other *vaqueros* across the road. For a moment longer the stranger studied those more distant men, and the *vaquero* directly in front of him. He spoke, softly. The *vaquero* shrugged without answer and remained watchfully facing the stranger.

"Face-down," murmured Paul Spencer.

Doria nodded. Whatever that *vaquero* had said, the initiative now lay with the stranger. He turned his head a little. Those other *vaqueros* down near the jailhouse were standing stonily looking up at him. The stranger slumped and turned to walk across in the direction of the men opposite the saloon, his mentor trailing after.

Without much doubt, those three opposite the saloon had taken a prisoner. They had done it without raising a gun. Doria let his breath out, slowly. "I wish to hell I knew what exactly was going on," he murmured, but Paul Spencer had already made up his mind.

"They just nabbed one of Alvarado's men, that's what's going on."

The *vaqueros* had their prisoner back in the shade. They disarmed him in plain sight of anyone who happened to be watching, then two faced the saloon again while the third one remained back beside the captive.

Spencer felt admiration. "Neat as clockwork. They didn't even raise their voices."

Doria said, "I'm going across the road to watch from over there." He pointed to a recessed doorway nearby. "Step in there, Paul, it'll protect you from both sides."

Two young boys rolling a discarded wagon-tire came down the roadway making boyish, piping sounds as they used sticks to keep their steel tire from wobbling out of control. They were trailed by a medium-sized brown dog who seemed to be enjoying this sport as much as the lads were. Otherwise, a man wearing a short, soiled apron emerged from a shop where saddles and harness were manufactured. He stood a moment looking up and down the roadway, then calmly spat into the dust and turned back into his shop.

Three riders appeared from the lower desert and rode up as far as the liverybarn where they rode in and swung off. They looked like ordinary desert cattlemen; their movements were slow and calm, as though they had no inkling there was trouble brewing.

When a hostler had led their horses inside to be cared for the rangemen started up in the direction of the saloon.

Doria watched from across the roadway as the three horsemen strode up past the recessed doorway, saw Spencer in there, looking twice, then suddenly stopped speaking among themselves as they turned and looked in the opposite direction where Doria was obviously waiting. They saw the *vaqueros* too, and the last hundred and fifty feet before they reached the saloon, their strides lengthened, their shoulders came up, and they lost their casual attitude. At the saloon they ducked inside swiftly leaving the roadway empty and hushed again.

The heat was rising even where there were shadows. Distantly, those boys with their discarded old steel tire were still audible in the hush.

Doria moved southward to a narrow place between two old mud buildings and felt a draft of cool air coming from back there. He leaned to look. The dog-trot was empty and as far back through as the alleyway he could see, there was no one.

He was straightening back around when one of the *vaqueros* left his companion south of the jailhouse and strolled up to say, "*Buenas dias.* I am the nephew of Calvo Sotelo. The ones you are looking for—we don't know where they are. And the other one from the east side of town—he slipped through the watchers over in Mex-town." The Mexican thinly smiled as he steadily regarded Jim Doria. "Behind me across the road and atop the general store we have a friend who is watching. He is the one who signaled with his bandana when that stranger came up from behind the stores. My friends up there saw the signal."

Doria's gaze lifted to the opposite rooftop but he saw no one. He looked at the tall *vaquero*. "Are you sure there are only four of them with Alvarado?"

"Yes. There was an old man who went south with his burro this morning to look for them. Maybe you saw him come back a while ago and say something to us as he walked past."

Doria nodded. He had indeed witnessed that little drama.

"The old man told us how many there were and that they were splitting up as they entered town." The *vaquero's* thin smile returned. "I told the old man to have a boy give you a note."

Doria studied the Mexican. He had lighter skin than many Mexicans, his features were not as coarse and his black eyes showed intelligence, resolution, and what Doria thought under different circumstances, might prove to be humor. "I guess we just wait," he said, and the *vaquero* agreed.

"*Si*. But for Alvarado this will be the end of the road. He has been here before, many times, but this is the first time he went after someone in Soledad who was not a fugitive. We always knew he was a bad man." The *vaquero* looked northward where the other three Mexicans were standing, with their captive, then he looked back at Jim Doria. "Alvarado was never a man who believed in the law. He only believed in Alvarado. We should have done this long ago."

Doria accepted the Mexican's statement and said, "His friend the deputy is locked in one of his own cells inside the jailhouse."

The *vaquero* looked a little surprised. He said, "Good. We wondered about him." Without another word the Mexican returned to where his friend had been standing. Doria saw them conversing quietly.

Spencer emerged from his recessed doorway to gaze enquiringly across the road where he had seen his partner conversing with the *vaquero*. Doria made a little reassuring gesture and Spencer looked around, then started back to the doorway, but stopped as a solitary horseman came into town from over on the west side. He emerged into the main thoroughfare from a little side-street, halted and sat looking around. Doria saw him then, when he was far enough away from the side-road to be visible. What Doria noticed even at that distance was the ivory gun-stock.

The horseman urged his mount out and walked down the roadway eyeing the loafing *vaqueros* opposite the saloon. He did not see Doria until he was farther along. Spencer turned slowly to watch and the rider also saw him. He studied Spencer for a long time before reining over in the direction of the jailhouse.

Now, finally, the town seemed to be purposefully quiet. Perhaps people had guessed there was some kind of trouble coming earlier, but until this moment the empty roadway and the quietness had not seemed deliberate. Now it did.

How people could know there was trouble was anyone's guess, but as Doria watched Alvarado ride past he thought perhaps the people over in Mex-town had passed along a whispered warning.

Alvarado turned when he was abreast of Doria, gazed at him, then shifted his glance to the pair of motionless *vaqueros*.

To Jim Doria the manhunter's bold appearance meant there probably would not be an attempt at bush-whacking. He knew Alvarado had seen his unarmed rider up there opposite the saloon with the three *vaqueros*. Alvarado would realize that the man had been captured but he gave no hint of this, nor did he even act as though he had recognized the unarmed man.

He turned in at the tie-rack out front of the jailhouse. Doria straightened up a little. If those two *vaqueros* moved to halt Alvarado from entering as they had done the other man who had tried it earlier, the Mex-ican informer, the showdown would probably occur. Doria hoped they would allow Alvarado to enter the jailhouse—and would then enter behind him. He would be boxed in and capture would be easier than it would be out in the roadway.

12
DEATH!

Jim Doria's error was in attributing to Carter Alvarado the direct reasoning process Doria himself might use. Alvarado was an altogether different kind of individual. His success as a paid manhunter had proved that many times. When he dismounted out front of the jailhouse and methodically looped both reins at the pole, he straightened up slowly and turned to glance around.

He knew he was being watched. He also had to know there were two men, at the very least, who would fight him. He looked over where Jim Doria was standing. They exchanged a long glance, then the manhunter turned slightly to glance toward the recessed doorway where Paul Spencer was grimly staring back at him.

Everything Alvarado did was methodical and deliberate. He had two *vaqueros* on his right, slightly to one side and behind him. There were those other three northward opposite the saloon.

What began to worry Doria a little was the man's absolute calm confidence. Ordinarily, no man, not even a very fast and accurate gunfighter, would behave as the black-eyed, stocky man was acting, and although Jim Doria only knew Alvarado by hearsay, he was prepared to believe the manhunter was anything but a fool.

Alvarado turned, eyed the pair of watchful *vaqueros* and spat, then he said, "It's up to you, *amigos.* It's not your fight and if you butt in . . . we have four hostages in Mex-town."

Doria heard every word as distinctly as though Alvarado had been speaking to him. He understood, now, why Carter Alvarado had chosen this bold approach. He had known the Mexicans were waiting for him, along with Spencer and Jim Doria. He had known it when he had ridden slowly down to tie up out front of the jailhouse, and he had just given his ultimatum.

Doria watched the *vaqueros.* The one who had said he was Calvo Sotelo's nephew, stood like stone for a long time, never once taking his eyes off Alvarado. The manhunter interpreted this stance the same way Jim Doria interpreted it: The *vaquero* had been caught unprepared. He was trying to adjust to being out-smarted. His stance indicated he was stubbornly considering the alternatives. Doria was fascinated by the man's situation, and while it occurred to him—as it no doubt had also occurred to the Mexican—that Alvarado could be lying, or bluffing, he could not make up his mind about this, and obviously, neither could the *vaquero.*

Again, though, Carter Alvarado demonstrated his cunning. He slowly reached inside a pocket, slowly withdrew his hand and pitched something into the dust at the *vaquero's* feet. It was a small gold crucifix on a delicate gold chain, the kind of object many Mexican women wore. Doria did not have to recognize the necklace. He knew that Alvarado had not been bluffing.

The *vaquero* stared, transfixed, at the dully shining object in the dust.

Jim Doria sensed that the *vaquero's* defiance was atrophying. He had only this one instance of Carter Alvarado's viciousness to convince him that all he had heard about the manhunter was true. It also occurred to him that if he allowed Alvarado to cow the *vaqueros,* the odds were going to abruptly shift against him—and his partner.

He ranged a quick look up along the overhead rooftops, saw no one, looked elsewhere, still saw no one, and decided it was now or never so he stepped away from the shaded storefront, gloves tucked under his shellbelt, and the moment he moved it attracted the manhunter's attention.

Alvarado turned on him. "You're Doria. I'm going to settle with you."

Doria had moved ahead just for that purpose. He did not say a word as he turned fully.

"You're in the sights of my men," Alvarado exclaimed with an edge to his voice. "One more step . . .!"

Paul Spencer had seen his partner's move and knew what it meant. He palmed his six-gun—and someone fired a carbine from the west side of the road. A chunk of adobe the size of a fist flew from the edge of the doorway. Spencer involuntarily flinched as he was bringing up his gun. He dropped flat one moment later. Doria saw this from the corner of his eyes as he turned sideways to present the narrowest target, and went for his gun.

Carter Alvarado had also planned against this. With one step he was beyond his horse so the animal was between them as he drew. Doria ducked sideways as the ivory-gripped Colt exploded.

Alvarado's horse gave a tremendous backward lunge, broke the reins which had been looped at the rack and stumbled in his frantic lunge to spin away. For this moment Carter Alvarado was exposed. Doria fired from the height of his belt, cocked and fired again. The second slug missed but the first one didn't and Alvarado, for all his cleverness, was punched backward under the impact. He fired into the ground three feet in front of himself as Doria's second bullet went wide.

That unseen man with the carbine fired too, but he evidently could not find Doria, being hidden over on the same side of the roadway, so he tried for another shot at Spencer. This bullet broke a store-window. The sound of tinkling glass mingled with the sudden shout of someone down near the liverybarn, where Doria's wild shot had perhaps come close enough to inspire someone into an outcry.

Alvarado fought to hold his balance and at the same time to swing up his gun again. Doria had him and he knew it; he raised his Colt a notch, steadied it perfectly and squeezed off his third shot. Carter Alvarado staggered drunkenly. Doria fired twice more, deliberately and without heeding his own peril.

Alvarado fell, his fancy-handled six-gun rolled from one hand, still cocked. Doria took a step to his right, closer to the front of the building. Someone fired at him with a six-gun from the west side of the road, but northward, between Doria and those three *vaqueros* shouted a warning to the other two *vaqueros* southward, who were evidently in the line of fire of the men across from the saloon.

Doria turned, looking for the man who had fired at him, but evidently the gunman had ducked into a dogtrot, or had already been in one and after that wild shot had ducked back again. Whatever had happened Doria could not see anyone up there, but those three *vaqueros* and their agitated unarmed captive.

He looked back. Alvarado had not moved, He was lying on his back staring straight up at the yellow sun.

Spencer jumped up and raced across the roadway. That carbine-man fired suddenly, levered up and fired again. Doria saw the gunsmoke, finally; the carbine-man was southward, down in the direction of the liverybarn but not quite that far south, and he too was using one of those narrow spaces between two buildings. His first shot had been wide but the second one dumped Paul Spencer in the thick dust close to the west side of the road, and as he fell Spencer roundly cursed, then rolled. Doria jumped ahead, grabbed cloth and wrenched his partner up against a storefront, left him and turned just as those two *vaqueros* south of the jailhouse fired almost at the same time.

They must have sighted the man with the carbine, but if they had hit him there was no sign of it. No one dropped forward into the sunlight.

Spencer was threshing around and cursing when Jim Doria darted to a dog-trot, jumped down it and raced for the narrow end where sunlight lay strongly where trash and a crooked alleyway were.

He sank to one knee waiting and watching, but if the man with the Winchester was still hidden in his dog-trot he evidently intended to remain there because no one emerged for the full length of the alley.

For several dead-silent minutes there was not a sound of any kind. Doria flung off sweat and continued to wait. The man with the carbine had either made good his escape before Doria had got back there, or he was still between two buildings. Doria's shirt was dark with salt-sweat even though he was not aware of it. There was a strong smell of burnt gunpowder in the hot, motionless atmosphere, but most noticeable of all was the silence. It seemed to be stretching out to an absolute limit.

Time dragged. Doria arose carefully, cocked gun ready, and walked carefully along the rear of the buildings southward. At each dog-trot he halted, waited, then got down low to peer around. Each one was empty, all the way down to the liverybarn. The man had escaped!

He waited out back of the liverybarn, listening, and when he had not heard anything more ominous than a stalled horse or two stamping at flies, he eased around into the gloomy, cool runway, and began working his way toward the front opening. He did not encounter a single person although he knew there was a liveryman and perhaps several hostlers somewhere around. Like every other prudent individual in Soledad this morning, they had suddenly become invisible.

The roadway, too was as sunbright and empty and quiet as it had been before, when Doria came to the front of the barn. Even those old men who had been sitting in sunshine were gone, but up near the jail-house several Mexicans were making Spencer comfortable upon a wooden bench—and Carter Alvarado had still not moved.

Doria stepped forth into plain sight. He kept moving though, for while he was willing to draw gunfire he was not willing to make himself too good a target. No one fired. No one appeared nor seemed to know who he was or what he was doing, although surely there were discreet spectators around the corners of a number of store-windows.

There were still two of Alvarado's men loose. The man using a Winchester had disappeared, and according to Doria's guess, he had been one of the pair to the west of town. If there had been another man with him, then there were still a pair of them some-where around—unless they had seen Alvarado killed, in which case they might have high-tailed it. But if Alvarado had been telling the truth about hostages in Mex-town, then there was a man over there. By Doria's estimate, wherever they were, there had to be two of them remaining, and possibly even three of them.

He walked up where Spencer was. Paul had one boot off. It was lying to one side of the bench and Paul glanced up at Doria with an enquiring glance. "Find him?"

Doria replied while looking at the bared foot. "No. Didn't see any sign of him. How bad off are you?"

Spencer pointed. "Shot the heel off my boot. It felt like my ankle went with it, but I guess it was just a bad twist." Spencer gently massaged the ankle, then he swore, and one of the *vaqueros* grinned.

Doria looked around. There were four *vaqueros*. The fifth one, the nephew of Calvo Sotelo, was missing. Doria asked Spencer if he could make out, and as Spencer answered affirmatively, he then moved as though to arise. "Hey! Wait, I'll go with you."

Doria shook his head. "Not this time, pardner."

"Then take a couple of these fellers with you," Spencer said quickly. "The odds are still against you."

Doria looked at the *vaqueros* who evidently had been unable to follow what had been said in English or perhaps what had been *thought* between the partners. They looked owlishly from Doria to Spencer and back again.

Doria winked at his partner. "You just set there— and worry. I'll be back directly."

"Yeah. On a flat plank!" As Doria turned to cross the road Spencer began exhorting the *vaqueros* to go with Doria. One of them finally turned and struck out. He wore a tied-down gun and was darker than the others. There was almost a villainous look about him.

Doria reached the far side of the roadway when those three rangemen who had ridden into town earlier, and who had ducked into the saloon, evidently feeling emboldened now that the gunfire seemed ended, peered over the saloon doors, then pushed on outside. They stood like logs watching Doria and the villainous-looking Mexican pass from sight down between two buildings on their way to Mex-town. Then the three rangemen glanced carefully all round before striking out in Spencer's direction.

Several other people also appeared, timidly, it seemed, and tentatively as though prepared to duck for cover on a moment's notice. They stood gawking down where the *vaqueros* and Spencer were, but only those three cowboys ventured down there.

The sun was high. It was in fact slightly off-center. There were no appreciable shadows and even where there were, the warmth was not mitigated at all as Doria came out behind the main section of Soledad into utter silence and sunlight, leavened only for as long as he remained with his back near one of the buildings at his back.

That villainous-looking *vaquero* stepped through, grinned and pointed as he rattled off something Doria could not understand. He beckoned for the Mexican to lead the way.

He knew where Sotelo's adobe was without a guide, but it appeared likely that if the *vaquero* preceded him

124

that manhunter who had the hostages might be at least temporarily lulled.

It was just a lean hope, because there were no more people abroad in Mex-town than there had been over in *gringo*-town.

Even the dogs seemed to have sensed something. But the chickens hadn't, they were still just as industriously scratching the hot, thin dirt as ever, unmindful of the two men going carefully northward among the adobe residences.

The *vaquero* halted near the glassless window of a humble house and lightly whistled. When a stunningly beautiful woman appeared, the *vaquero* spoke so fast it seemed to Doria all the man's words ran together. But the beautiful woman seemed to understand. She looked beyond, where Doria was looking back, and softly replied to the *vaquero*. As he started carefully around the little house the beautiful woman watched Doria. He moved closer. She was flawless, what he could see of her over the high, recessed windowsill. He smiled. She smiled back, then said in lightly accented English, "Your companion does not speak English. Do you speak Spanish?"

Doria paused to answer. "No ma'm." He looked directly at her. "But I could sure learn it, lady, if you were teaching it."

The beautiful woman laughed and disappeared. It was like listening to cold water over shiny rocks on a hot day, that laughter. He turned and went looking for his guide. The *vaquero* was around in front of the small adobe, motionless and watching. In the middle distance was the old mud church where Calvo Sotelo and several other older men tended a garden patch. Nearer, utterly still in the hot sunlight was the house of Calvo Sotelo. The *vaquero* pointed to the house, then shook his head and muttered something. He shifted his arm to indicate the old church and said, *"Alli,"* his pronunciation soft: "Ayee."

Doria looked at the church. It was as still and abandoned-looking as most of the buildings roundabout also were. "In the church?" he said, not believing he had understood. The *vaquero* studied Doria's face, *"Si, Señor, alli."*

He looked back, then muttered to himself that if this man knew what he was talking about Doria would eat his hat. But he smiled and the *vaquero* smiled back. His face did not look as villainous when he smiled.

If the manhunter had his hostages in the church . . . Doria looked perplexedly at the *vaquero* again. "You're plumb sure he's got them in there?"

The *vaquero* said nothing but continued to smile. Why, he groaned to himself, of five *vaqueros* did he have to get saddled with one who couldn't speak English. But maybe it would work out. He tapped the man's shoulder and made a gesture to move ahead.

The *vaquero* did not so much as hesitate. Also, he knew this area because he back-tracked, then cut around through the little houses until he came to a worn and crumbling adobe wall which was waist high. Without looking back he ducked forward and scuttled along out of sight from anyone upon the opposite side of the wall. But Doria had seen no one beyond; all he had seen was a neatly weeded area where vegetables and gourds seemed to be growing very profusely. Still, he ducked forward and went scuttling behind his guide.

13
EULALIA

To Jim Doria it did not make sense, using a big old adobe church as a place to hold hostages, and as he craftily straightened up at the far end of the ancient adobe wall to peer across, he kept thinking that there had been *two* men who had fired at him around on Main Street; the man with the Winchester, and once, a man with a handgun across the road.

Now—if there were hostages inside that church, there had to be *three* enemies left, not just two, and if that were so, then Alvarado had returned with five men, including himself, not four men.

His guide tapped Doria's arm and pointed to a corner of the long, perpetually shaded veranda all along the rear wall of the old church, then he struck out for it in a running crouch.

There was cover all the way. There was also heat right up until they reached the corner of the old church, and up there the roofline hung two feet beyond the wall, which was customary among adobe buildings in order to prevent erosion from rainfall. In this hot shade the two men stood pressed to the rough-textured old wall, waiting, although Doria had no idea what they were waiting for.

His companion grinned, and that was something else Doria did not see much reason for.

It seemed an interminable wait and each time Doria expressed impatience, the Mexican's grin grew wider. Doria gave up.

Moments later he responded to a light tap from the Mexican. They turned up along the windowless high north wall, went almost to the farther corner, then halted when a man's laugh, low and suggestive, came from somewhere around front. The *vaquero* halted. He reached down and brought up his right hand with a thin, light knife with a double-edged blade which shone in the shaded daylight.

Doria felt as though he were merely a spectator, someone who had followed along just to observe. But he palmed his Colt.

That man's throaty, soft laughter died. Doria had to strain to hear it, but there were voices around there, indistinct and so quiet it was almost impossible to hear them without straining.

Then a woman laughed. It was like music at dusk. Doria straightened instantly. He recognized that sound. The exquisite woman from the window in the little adobe house!

Now, finally, Doria began to understand what his companion had done, what he had been discussing with the beautiful woman at the window. She was the bait!

128

He gently shook his head. He did not know the man-hunter around there, had never seen him, but he could understand exactly how that man felt at this moment. He almost felt pity for the man. Almost.

His companion removed his wide-brimmed hat, sank to one knee and eased part of his face around the rough wall, remained for a moment in that position, then gradually pulled back and soundlessly arose. He turned and gestured for Doria to step up and do the same thing. Doria obeyed.

The man around at the front steps of the church was standing with his back to Doria, half in shade from the high overhang, and half in sunlight where those broad, low stone steps led to the recessed front entry-way to the church.

The man had a Winchester hooked in one arm and a tied-down six-gun around his middle. He had a strong, wide back and muscular sloping shoulders, but that was all Doria saw. His attention was drawn beyond the manhunter. That beautiful woman was also half in shadows and half in sunlight. She was handsomely proportioned, tall for a Mexican woman, with hair so black the sunlight got caught in it making blue lights. Her blouse had a wide neck to show golden arms and shoulders. She glanced just once past the manhunter, saw Doria, did not even blink as she brought her black, liquid soft gaze back to the manhunter.

The man said, "I wasn't worried. I knew Alvarado would take them out. It just seemed like a lot of gun-fire for killin' two men, that was all."

The woman's full, heavy mouth was softly lifted in a smile as she replied in English with only the barest trace of an accent. "He is a man people know. A famous man on the south desert."

The manhunter offered a quick retort. "*Señorita,* I'm pretty well-known too, over in west Texas. In a year or so I'll maybe even be as famous as Carter Alvarado."

The woman's beautiful eyes softened. "I believe you." She glanced almost casually at the church-front. "How long will you keep those people in there?"

"Until Alvarado comes along and tells me it's all right to let them go. We only need them to make damned sure no one from Mex-town don't get big ideas."

"Do you have the old man in there?"

"Sotelo? Naw, he's hurt too bad to move."

"You shot him then?"

The man's voice turned oily, turned low and heavy. "No. Alvarado shot him. He dang near missed because the old bastard tried to run out of a cave up in one of those brushy canyons. I wouldn't shoot him. He might be related to you, and I wouldn't touch no one close to you . . . You could come inside with me."

She cocked her head slightly. "Then, they might escape while you were with me."

"Naw, I got 'em all tied. Seven of 'em, women and kids mostly. They won't try nothing." The manhunter straightened up, evidently in anticipation. His voice changed slightly. "There are a lot of little rooms in there. We could be alone in one of them."

Doria's grip on his six-gun tightened. There was sweat on his palm and also on his face. The *vaquero* tapped his shoulder, tapped it insistently and finally when Doria turned the Mexican shook his head and motioned Doria away. He must have sensed the anger in the *gringo*, or perhaps he had seen Doria's body tightening. In either case he insistently gestured for Doria to get out of the way.

The Mexican eased past shouldering Doria back away, then the Mexican leaned from a standing position, looked around, moved his head sideways in a signal to the beautiful woman. Without another sound the *vaquero* stepped around the corner, right arm coming up in a practiced, fluid gesture. He hurled the knife.

Doria, with no experience at something like this, had a moment to reflect upon the possible inaccuracy, and the armed man's immediate response with his guns if the Mexican missed.

But the knife did not miss. Doria heard a choking sound, almost like a deep-down wet cough, then he also heard a carbine strike the worn stone steps and a moment later a duller, more solid sound.

Doria stepped swiftly around where he could see, gun rising as he moved into plain sight.

That manhunter was lying on his side in a position of sleep. The hilt of the *vaquero's* double-edged knife was protruding from the manhunter's back between the shoulders. It did not seem that a knife-blade could have gone so deeply. The throw had not appeared to

Doria to have that much power behind it, but Doria had never seen a knife thrown with deadly intent before.

The beautiful woman's face had lost color. She looked from the dead man to the *vaquero*. But her mouth was toughly set and her clasped hands seemed to be loose. The *vaquero* stooped to pluck away the dead man's weapons. He tossed them back toward the corner of the building, then straightened up to say something curt to the beautiful woman in harsh Spanish. She did not move nor acknowledge whatever he had told her, as the *vaquero* turned and jerked his head at Doria.

The woman said, "He wants you to remain out here in case another of them comes. He is going inside to free the hostages and take them out the back way." She raised her eyes to Doria. They looked larger and darker in the sudden paleness of her face.

Doria nodded at the *vaquero,* and to indicate understanding he said, *"Si,"* which was almost the full extent of his knowledge of the Spanish language.

The *vaquero* turned swiftly away. He was a man of supple, muscular, resolute movement. Within moments he had passed beyond the large, very old double doors to disappear inside where it was cool and gloomy and faintly aromatic from centuries of waving censers.

Doria moved between the dead manhunter and the beautiful woman to cut off her view of the corpse. He holstered his Colt. There were benches up along the sheltered, shaded front of the church. Over there, she would probably not be able to see around the front abutment where the corpse was lying so he took her back there and eased her down upon a bench.

He had a perfect view out front and in both directions as he remained standing.

The woman shuddered as though from cold, except that it was almost as warm back where they were as it was out in the sunlight.

The voices of people inside the old church came mutedly out where Doria and the handsome woman were. He did not understand what few scraps of quick, worried Spanish he heard but the woman looked up and smiled slightly as she said, "Perez is a hero."

He smiled. "Perez is his name?"

"You didn't know his name?"

Doria shrugged. "I can't even talk to him let alone ask what his name is."

She kept looking up. "You have a name?"

"Jim Doria."

"Doria? Is it a Spanish name?"

Not that he knew of. It didn't sound very Spanish to him, but then he was an orphan. "I guess not," he told her, and at the odd look he got from her he explained. "I never knew my folks. I was raised in an orphanage in Council Bluffs and ran away when I was thirteen." He turned to look out and around. It made him uncomfortable to talk about himself. He never did it, if there was a way to avoid it. When he looked back she was still looking at him, so he said, "I spent most of my life up in the Montana, Wyoming, Colorado country. Except for coming down through here—near here anyway—a time or two."

Her gaze did not waver. "On your way down to Mexico?"

He reddened slightly but it was not noticeable under his normally bronzed shading. "Yeah. A time or two."

She shifted her gaze, and he understood. She knew he was an outlaw. Then she said, "I grew up five hundred miles from here. My parents died in an epidemic one hot summer. I came to Soledad to live with an aunt and uncle. Now they are also dead—three years ago." She looked up again. "I don't like the south desert. Someday I'll go back north where there are trees and grass—and water." She suddenly stood up. "I had better go around back where Perez will be."

Doria took down a big breath. "Ma'm. One question before you go . . ."

"My name? It is Eulalia Montoya."

That hadn't been what he had been about to ask. "Are you married?"

She looked straight at him, shook her head, then turned to walk away.

They had only been together alone out in front of the church for a few minutes, and now as she disappeared around the far corner of the church, Doria reached up to tilt his hat back, then he slowly turned, gazed at the man with the knife-hilt showing in the center of his back, and blew out a gusty breath. One moment later a solitary gunshot rang out from over in the main part of town and Doria instinctively stepped back into the shade with a thick adobe wall partially in front.

There was no second gunshot and the silence returned.

Perez came briskly around the same corner Eulalia Montoya had disappeared around. He was looking left and right with an enquiring expression on his face. He rattled off something in Spanish which Jim Doria assumed had to do with that gunshot, so Doria pointed. "From over yonder," he said. "From over where we left my partner."

The *vaquero* nodded as though he understood, which he probably did. He jerked his head and Doria struck out beside him. Once, he looked back. All he saw was a short, heavy woman dressed in black standing by an adobe house looking after them. The woman raised her right hand to cross herself.

They got back up through one of the dog-trots and halted far enough back to be unseen while they studied the empty, hot roadway. There was no one out there, not even those *vaqueros* who had been with Spencer. There was no sign of Spencer either although his empty discarded boot with the blown-off heel was lying near the bench, looking forlorn and useless.

Perez turned. Doria edged around him, stepped out of the passageway and waited a moment. If anyone saw him they gave no indication of it. He studied doorways and shadows upon the opposite side of the roadway, then stepped forth to cross over. Perez hitched at his shellbelt and trudged along behind, his dark face intent, black eyes missing nothing.

14
THE LAW

There were two dead men stretched out upon the earthen floor of the jailhouse. One was Carter Alvarado, the other corpse was that deputy sheriff Doria and Spencer had locked in a cell.

There were three rangemen in the room and three *vaqueros*. When Perez and Doria entered they all looked up but for a moment no one spoke. Then Perez rattled off a question in Spanish and one of the *vaqueros* rattled back a curt answer. None of this helped Doria's understanding of what had happened.

Spencer came limping up out of the cell-room, saw his partner and pulled a crooked little mirthless grin. "That son of a bitch got out," he said, pointing to the dead deputy. He held up a little thong. "He had a key hidden in the cell." Spencer hobbled to a bench and sank down. "He got out before you shot Alvarado. He was across the road. It was him shot at you with the handgun. Then he got foolish and after you walked over to Mex-town, the darned fool tried to get a horse at the liverybarn." Spencer pointed to one of the *vaqueros*. "That feller was down there because he figured someone might try getting away. The deputy drew but the *vaquero* was faster." Spencer paused to gaze at the dead lawman. "They dragged him up here." Spencer glanced up again. "You find that other one?"

"Yeah."

"You captured him?"

"No. This feller killed him with a knife."

The three silent rangemen and Paul Spencer stared at Perez, who may not have understood the words, but he understood the looks he was getting. *Gringos* did not look favorably upon knifings, even when they thought they were probably justified.

Spencer said, "There's still one around here somewhere. That feller with the carbine."

One of the dusty rangemen made a dry comment. "Not unless he's an idiot, he ain't still around here. He's probably five miles off and riding like the wind."

Spencer shrugged. "I just locked up the prisoner. He sure is scairt. He saw Alvarado get it and now he's in that cell sweatin' bullets for fear we'll hang him. I'm willing."

A large-boned graying man with hard eyes and a lined face, studied Doria without saying a word. He scarcely took his eyes off Doria as the *vaqueros* began edging toward the door. Perez said something to them. One of them turned to face Doria. "We go now. It's been done. It should have been done long ago."

Doria nodded at the man. "Your people are all right. Perez turned them loose." He smiled at the *vaqueros*. "Thanks. You fellers made all the difference. We're right obliged. If you see Calvo Sotelo, tell him we'll be along directly—with a jug of wine."

After the Mexicans had departed, the little jailhouse office still seemed crowded. One of those dusty

137

rangemen went to a chair and as he sat down he said, "Mister Doria, you sure took some long chances."

Spencer snorted. "He's always doin' stuff like that. Sometimes I wonder how he's kept alive as long as he has."

The hard-eyed graying man spoke next. "Anyone get hurt over in Mex-town except that feller who got knifed."

Doria shook his head, trying to make up his mind about this rangeman. "No; got hell scairt out of them is all. Except for the old gent Alvarado shot. He didn't look too good but he's a tough old cuss. He'll make it, most likely." Doria and the graying man looked steadily at one another, then Doria said, "You fellers run cattle down here?"

The other pair of rangemen said nothing, clearly leaving the answer to the hard-faced older man. For a moment this rangeman did not reply, then he moved toward the open door as he said, "Would you mind steppin' outside with me for a minute, Mister Doria?"

Spencer looked quizzically at the graying man then shrugged as Doria and the older man passed out of the office. "How about one of you fellers lookin' around here," he said to the remaining pair of rangemen. "There's got to be a bottle of whisky cached in the desk or in a cupboard."

Outside, the sun was moving westerly, the thin shadows were beginning to firm up, to broaden and deepen. It was still hot and would remain so long after the sun had set, but there was coolness to the shade, finally, and it was into one of those pleasant places where the graying man moved to turn, finally, facing the empty roadway as he cocked one booted foot behind himself on the adobe jailhouse wall. He stood a moment in grave contemplation of his surroundings, thumbs hooked in his gunbelt, one fist closed, the other open.

"Ugly damned town," he murmured casually. "I've been all along this border country and I've only seen three or four of these old towns that got enough water to grow trees and maybe a patch of squash." He looked at Jim Doria. "You like this country?"

Doria half smiled in spite of himself. "Beats the inside of a jail," he replied, and the hard-eyed man also half-smiled.

"I guess it does at that." He raised his closed fist and gently opened it. There was a metal circlet on his palm with a steel star inside it. The letters on the circlet said U.S. Deputy Marshal.

Doria blinked but otherwise showed none of the surprise he felt.

"It's been a hell of a long, dusty trail, Mister Doria. My name is Joshua Logan. I work out of Las Crucas, some of the time, but my main headquarters is up in Denver. The other two deputy marshals with me—the three of us hauled our horses on a train as far as Rosario, and took up the trail from there."

Marshal Logan dropped the badge into a shirt pocket and continued to stand relaxed with one leg cocked up, while he returned to studying the storefronts across the roadway. "In another month it'll be hot enough down here to fry eggs on the rocks . . . We didn't trail you as much as we trailed Alvarado. He's another one's been on our books for a long time . . . We followed him over the line down to Santa Maria . . . Did you know he lost two of his men down there?"

Doria looked at Logan. "Lost them?"

"Yeah. Ironic justice, I guess a man could call it. They bought into a poker game down there—using iron pyrites for gold. They lost, and when they paid up one of the other players recognized fool's gold when he saw it. There was a fight. Alvarado's lads come off second best. They was bein' buried when we rode in, and Alvarado was frothin' at the mouth and trying his damndest to find you fellers. He figured you'd done that some way . . . Mister Doria, I don't figure Alvarado would have rode right down the roadway here to kill you fellers if he hadn't been so mad he wasn't thinkin' straight."

Joshua Logan straightened his bent leg and hauled up off the wall. "You saved us a job, here, Mister Doria. From what we picked up from that prisoner in the cells, you fellers was tryin' to help an old Messican who had helped you fellers. Is that about how it happened?"

"About," agreed Doria, laconically, and exchanged a look with the hard-eyed older man. "We figured that son of a bitch would go back and raise hell, but we didn't think he'd be able to find Sotelo. Then we saw those two fellers with little tobacco sacks of gold down in Santa Maria, and guessed they'd found the gent."

"And you came back to lend a hand?"

"Well, the old gent was right good to us and right at that time we sure needed a friend."

Logan lightly scratched the tip of his nose. "You should have stayed down in Santa Maria."

Doria could not dispute that. Not now anyway. "I guess we should have, Mister Logan. But when a man does you a favor and risks his own hide doing it, you owe him, don't you?"

"Yes. I feel like you owe him."

Up the road that man with the soiled apron stepped forth looking quickly around, then, instead of ducking back inside, he remained out there in the afternoon shade gazing down in the direction of the jailhouse. Another man walked forth. From across the road and northward, out of the saloon where Doria had first seen those three rangemen duck inside when he had thought they were desert cattlemen.

"Mister Doria," said Joshua Logan, "You and Mister Spencer rode the ranges up north for five years. Is that right?"

It was. It also indicated that Marshal Logan hadn't just loaded horses into a cattle-car, he had also done some reading up in Denver, and he had also perhaps asked some questions on the way south.

"For darn near six years, Mister Logan, and after that," replied Jim Doria, "We tried our hand at—other things."

Logan gravely inclined his head. "Yeah. You tried to rob a stagecoach near Laramie." Logan assumed a slightly amused expression. "The gunguard saw you before the stage stopped."

Doria reddened. "That son of a gun had more guns in more hands than a centipede. We was lucky to get out of that alive."

Logan chuckled. "Yeah. I talked to that driver and gunguard, they told me the last they saw of you and Mister Spencer you was scramblin' over rocks like lizards on a hot tin roof . . . The next time you stole two horses and they chased you southward. You made it into Mexico that time—with the horses."

Doria tilted his hat down to protect his eyes from what shafts of bright sunlight were still being reflected from the roadway. "Two fifty dollar horses," he muttered. "But it wasn't Paul with me that time. It was another feller. And he quit. We had to work too hard for too little money, he said."

Marshal Logan produced a plug of chewing tobacco and chivalrously offered Doria first gnaw. Doria refused and the lawman worried off a chew, pouched it and pocketed the ragged plug. He spat aside, shifted his cud and said, "You still think it pays, Mister Doria?"

There was ten thousand dollars in a saddlebag upon a horse tied in an old shed in back of town to influence Doria in hanging-fire before replying to that question.

"I expect it would pay if a man didn't get caught, and if he didn't have to live out of a dirty fryin' pan

142

and hide so much of the time, Mister Logan. And work so darn hard for his money . . . *Maybe* then it would pay, but to be right frank with you, Spencer and I been discussing that."

"And what does Spencer think?"

"He don't like it. He told me several times we should have stuck to riding for a living. Working the ranges and riding our own horses."

Logan spat then inclined his head. "He's plumb right, Mister Doria . . . In my experience, and I been at this business a long time, there are some fellers cut out to be outlaws, and some which aren't no matter how hard they work at it. . . . You fellers aren't." Logan chewed a moment, spat again, then turned to face Doria. "You lost this time too."

Doria did not say a word. He had no doubt but that he could beat this tough old deputy U.S. marshal to the draw. But there were two more of them inside keeping an eye on his partner. It wasn't even a very good stand-off. The edge lay with the three lawmen.

Then Logan's tough, ironic expression deepened as he spoke again. "That ten thousand dollars . . . is not worth a damn."

Doria stared.

"Counterfeit Mister Doria. They was holding it at the bank in Rosario for the U.S. Marshal in Denver as evidence against a ring of counterfeiters we busted loose last autumn."

Doria swallowed, hard, but did not utter a sound.

Logan continued to chew and gaze calmly at the

younger man. "That's the gospel truth. Maybe you boys could have spent it down in Mexico—but sooner or later even the Mexicans would have found out—then you probably would have ended up like Alvarado's two men did down there. And you'd have left a wide trail up here for us to follow if you'd come back to the U.S. to spend it . . . That's what I meant when I said some fellers just aren't cut out for bein' real outlaws . . . Care to walk up the road to the saloon with me and have some beer? Down here they call it *cerveza.*"

Doria had not moved. He still remained rooted as he said, "Counterfeit?"

"Every blessed note of it," affirmed the amused lawman.

Doria remained rooted to the ground. Across the road several townsmen had gathered to talk, but neither Doria nor the federal lawmen heeded them. Elsewhere, the town was beginning to show life again, more and more people ventured out.

Doria said, "Gawddammit! My partner's going to raise hell and prop it up."

Logan was amusedly sympathetic. "I don't know as I blame him. I guess I could have told him, but I wanted to meet you first, and now I'm glad I didn't tell him. You can do it."

Doria responded sourly. "Thanks. Thanks a hell of a lot." He studied the lawman. "Are you absolutely sure that's counterfeit money? It looked good to me, new and crisp and all."

"Just like it looked when they finished making it, Mister Doria. If you got some in your pocket I'll show you how we found out it was bogus."

Doria didn't have any of it. "It's in my saddlebags. We didn't spend any of it."

"Take one of those notes and rub it between your fingers. The ink comes off," said Logan. "Care to show me where it is? I'll show you how fake it is."

Doria considered. If it *was* useless money, then it would make no difference if he showed the lawman, and if it *wasn't* counterfeit and he was alone in the old shed with Logan, he could beat him to the draw, he was also confident of that. He jerked his head. "Come along."

The day was waning, people were staring curiously at Logan and Doria as the two men walked briskly up the roadway, then cut down toward the back alley. Those merchants who had been busily conversing across the road had finally arrived at a decision and were now heading across to the jailhouse. Four Mexicans carrying something which looked like the limp shape of a human being which was shrouded in an old black blanket came through from out back, and also headed for the jailhouse. Doria saw none of this. He had something far more important on his mind as he and Marshal Logan headed for the horse-shed in the golden, waning light of a dying day.

15
LAS CRUCAS

Paul Spencer could not believe it. "Banks don't keep counterfeit money."

"For evidence," explained Doria, and repeated what the deputy U.S. marshal had told him.

Spencer did not relent for one moment. "U.S. deputy marshal my butt," he exclaimed. "That old buzzard is a crook and he's tryin' to get our cache. Where is he, the darned old—?"

"He went over to Mex-town to talk to folks but he left his two shadows out front, one across the road by the general store."

"Watchin' this here jailhouse?"

"Yeah."

"So we're buttoned up in here."

Doria was becoming a little impatient. "It's the money I'm worried about, Paul."

Spencer nodded briskly and said, "I just told you. Those fellers aren't any more lawmen than I am, but they made you believe it. Then they came up with this silly story about counterfeit money."

Doria shook his head. "Paul, it is bogus money."

Spencer snorted. "Prove it by gawd!"

Doria pulled a crumpled greenback from his trouser pocket and another one from his shirt-pocket. He handed both to his partner, one in each hand, then he said, "Rub . . . Go ahead and rub each of them between your fingers . . . Well, damn it, don't just sit there—rub!"

Spencer worked his fingers industriously for a moment. He held up his left hand and his right one, then he very slowly lowered the left one and raised his eyes. "This here one smudged. I got the color on my . . . Jim; is this here the bogus one?"

"Yeah, partner, and we got ten thousand dollars worth of them."

Doria went to a chair, sat down and started making a cigarette. Across from him, his swollen ankle half again as large as the sound ankle in its scuffed old boot, Paul Spencer examined the two pieces of money, making comparisons of both sides, rubbing off more ink and finally saying, "Hell; it's just about impossible to tell 'em apart."

Doria trickled smoke. "That's the idea. What'd be the sense of making something folks would certainly know was counterfeit." Doria looked out of the doorway where late-day was settling, then he looked back. "Ten thousand dollars worth of it. There goes that little saloon you was going to buy, and there goes the foothill cow-ranch I been thinkin' about." Doria pointed. "That note you got in your hand—the good one—that's just about every blessed cent I got in the world."

Spencer dropped both hands to his lap. "What about the lawman?"

Clearly, now that he had been convinced about their imitation money, it was easier for Spencer to believe

147

the rest of it. Doria slumped as he replied. "He came after us all the way from Denver by way of Rosario. They had a telegraph office up there."

"You said they didn't."

"Well, I looked and I didn't see one," Doria retorted defensively. "Anyway, they're watching this building from out front, and there are three of them."

Spencer gingerly wiggled the toes of his wrenched ankle. Wiggled them again as he sat in scowling thought. "I had enough," he asserted eventually. "Take the chance on gettin' shot robbin' a damned bank, then hidin' and ridin' and skulkin' and going hungry and all." He looked up. "For a saddlebag full of paper we can't even give away. By gawd I had enough, Jim. If I never make more'n ten dollars a month again, for the rest of my life, I'm still goin' back to workin' the cow ranges. If you got a lick of sense left you'll do the same."

Doria looked straight across the room. "When? When do we go back to riding the range, Paul—ten years from now when we get out of prison?"

Spencer's toes stopped wiggling.

One of the dusty, rawhide-tough deputy marshals poked his head in from out front and asked if anyone had a match. Doria tossed him several and the deputy marshal pulled back to continue his comfortable vigil from out front.

Spencer said, "You know—I'm hungry enough to gnaw the tail feathers off a buzzard. You expect they'll shoot us if we walk out of here making for the café?"

They arose. Spencer had a stick with a cane-like handle to it he had found somewhere, but while this helped it did not help a whole lot. Walking for him was very painful. Doria offered an arm but Spencer frowned and struggled along by himself.

Outside, the two deputy U.S. lawmen watched without saying anything or making a move. They clearly did not really have much to worry about, obviously, as long as Spencer and Doria were on foot anyway.

The café was empty and its pale and paunchy proprietor was dozing, but he could not have dozed for long this late in the day so when he roused he smiled at his first supper customers and said, "Glad you boys made it. From the talk that's been goin' up an' down the back alleys today, you fellers sure had big odds against you."

Spencer looked without appreciation at the caféman. "Coffee, friend," he said, "and whatever you got for supper—just lots of it."

That graying deputy U.S. marshal entered removing his hat and gazing at the only two men along the eating counter with no show of surprise. He eased down, looked longest at Spencer, as though he were curious about how Spencer had taken the news that they had gone through so much for bogus money, then he glanced past at Doria, and nodded.

"Just come from Sotelo's place," he stated, beginning to search for the caféman. "And they say he's going to make it. Take a long time—feller his age an' all—but they're confident he'll make it . . . Where in hell is the cook?" Marshal Logan thumped the bartop so hard the pie table quivered and it was ten feet away.

He got action. That pale caféman came from behind a curtain which hid his cooking area and he was mad. "Which one of you thumped that counter?"

Logan answered. "I did. And by gawd I'll do it again unless you get some grub out here!"

The caféman turned red. For a moment he stood perfectly still, glaring, then he ducked under his counter with a savage curse. Doria leaned and waited. As the caféman's arm came up with the weapon Doria seized his wrist. They silently pitted strength in their struggle and Doria won. He removed the weapon and pushed the caféman back. In a tired voice he said, "Friend, just feed him, will you? Just feed us all."

The caféman was rigid with rage but Logan did not speak again and neither did the other two patrons at his counter, so eventually his anger burned down enough for him to turn and stamp back behind the curtain.

Doria gazed at Marshal Logan. "Everybody don't jump when a deputy U.S. marshal walks in, Mister Logan . . . What did you learn over in Mex-town?"

Logan continued to gaze at the curtain behind which that angry caféman had disappeared as he replied. "I learned you fellers helped Sotelo, and that Doria and a Mex named Perez got the hostages away safely, and that the deputy here in Soledad—Mike Curtis—has been intimidating Mexicans as often as he dared to for

a long while, making them hand over money for pro-
tection—and they aren't sad to see him cleaned out
permanently."

The caféman appeared, served Spencer and Doria,
glared at Marshal Logan and went back behind his
curtain. The lawman softly drummed on the coun-
tertop, narrowed hard gaze fixed upon the curtain.
"Coffee!" he bellowed, then turned to Spencer and
Doria again. "And the head honchos here in Soledad
want to know if you fellers would be interested in
taking over the lawman's job. They got up a com-
mittee to bury Alvarado and Mike Curtis the deputy.
They asked me if you fellers would be interested."

Doria and Spencer stared until the caféman had
brought coffee, had glared, and had then departed.

Spencer said, "Mister, I wouldn't be a lawman for
all the money on earth!"

Marshal Logan was not offended. He lit into his meal
as he said, "I told them that was about what you would
say. I didn't tell them you were bank-robbers . . . This
here meat is as tough as the skirt off an old saddle." He
chewed, and chewed, then shook his head. "Mister
Doria, I'm supposed to tell you they want to see you
over at Sotelo's place." He chewed a little longer,
swallowed with an exaggerated effort, then also said,
"Don't leave town. All right?"

Doria nodded. "All right."

Spencer was not that docile. "Why shouldn't we
leave town—if we can?"

Logan sawed at another piece of meat. "Because it'll

just make more work for me and I've already done enough horse-backing catching up to you boys, and if I have to do it again I'm going to be disagreeable. And besides that—you're prisoners." He chewed, thought, then said, "Sort-of prisoners." He looked at Doria. "They're waitin' for you at the Sotelo place."

After Doria had departed Paul Spencer wrinkled his brow. "What is a sort-of prisoner?"

"A sort-of prisoner," explained the federal marshal, "is a feller I don't really want to haul back with me to Denver. They're usually more damned fools than outlaws. I been culling them out for fifteen years and I've never been wrong." He looked at Spencer. "You like bein' an outlaw?"

"No. In fact *hell no!*"

"You figure when you ride out of Soledad to get back at it again?"

"Not on your tintype," retorted Spencer. "All I got out of it is trouble and danger and a lot of confounded discomfort. I'm goin' back to punching cows—and so is Jim Doria—the idiot!"

"That," explained Marshal Logan, "is a sort-of outlaw." Then he went back to eating, grimacing and rolling his eyes.

Doria, who walked from the café through cooling early evening through a dog-trot to Mex-town and headed for the Sotelo adobe, was also pondering that designation—sort-of outlaw. He did not see the supple figure move to intercept him near a small adobe until she said his name, then he halted.

She was now wearing a white blouse, which she abundantly filled out. Her skirt was tight at the waist but full to the ankles. Her arms and throat were bare in the soft shadows and she smiled.

Doria smiled back, then softly wagged his head. He had never in his life seen anything like her. "I'm going over to see Calvo Sotelo," he explained to her. "Care to come along?"

She hesitated briefly, then said, "He is sleeping. I was just over there. His daughter and nephew are taking care of him. He is gaining strength, but right now he is sleeping."

"Sure wouldn't want to waken a man who needs his rest," stated Doria, gazing steadily at her.

Her smile lingered. "I'm sure you wouldn't. Did you know the big deputy marshal isn't going to arrest you and your partner?"

"He isn't?"

"No. He told us that before he left the Sotelo *jacal.*"

"Did he say why he wasn't going to?"

"No. But he laughed—it was something about money, he said, then I left." She gazed at him. "He told us about Deputy Curtis." She paused again. "Will you walk with me to the church?"

He moved close and they strolled side by side. She smelled of some kind of flower. He didn't know what scent it was but he liked it. He screwed up his courage. "Eulalia, when are you going north?"

"Soon. Does it matter?"

"Yes, it matters."

They halted near the dark rear verandah of the old church. She turned. "You are also going north?"

"Yeah. If I'm free I am."

"Where—north?"

He grinned at her. "Wherever you're going."

"Las Crucas."

"Yeah. I always wanted to see Las Crucas."

"What have you heard about it?"

He said, "Nothing."

She cocked her head a little. "Then why do you want to see it?"

"Because you'll be there."

She studied him, then laughed and he laughed with her.

They went along the verandah out back to an old wooden bench. She sat down and looked up at him. "You are married?"

"Nope. Never have been. Never even thought much about it," he answered sitting down at her side.

"And—your trade?"

He sighed and dropped his hat upon the bench at his far side. "Range-riding. Pure and simple range-riding. Nothing else ever again."

She studied his profile. "I have a thousand acres at Las Crucas. My parents owned it. My father had cattle a long time ago. It is good grassland."

He turned slowly. "You own it?"

"Yes. It is leased to a cowman. The income from it is what I live on."

"Good grassland—with water and trees?"

"*Si*. But very run down. The fences and the buildings are old and run down."

He studied her in the shadows. She was beautiful, and full-figured. "A woman can't run much of a cow outfit by herself, Eulalia."

Her black eyes twinkled. "It is a fact, *Señor.*"

"I'd hire out real cheap. Just beans and keep. And I work hard and know the business."

"How cheap do you work?" she asked softly.

He kept looking at her. "For you—one smile in the morning and one in the evening, and on Sundays a laugh—the same laugh I heard when you spoke to Perez the first time I saw you."

She slid her gaze away and sat a while motionless and silent. Then she turned back and said, "You are sure you are not married?"

He was surprised. "Not that I know of, I'm not, but . . . ."

"But . . . ?"

"But I'm just about willing to be married."

Maybe she blushed. It was too dark to tell. "I think I'll hire you. One smile in the morning and one at night." She looked down and smoothed her skirt. It was the first indication she had given so far that she could be embarrassed.

He said, "You're beautiful. You've been told that before. But you really are."

Without looking up she softly said, "For a Mexican?"

"For *anyone*. What's Mexican got to do with it?"

"For me, it has nothing to do with it," she murmured, and raised her face. "To you . . . ?"

He leaned back and blew out a soft sigh. "We got to get to know each other, Eulalia."

"Yes, I think so, Jim."

"And when we get to know each other I want to tell you something that hit me like a ton of rocks the first time I saw you."

She stood up. "Then let's wait until we do know one another better, Jim." She waited until he was on his feet, then started slowly back through the warm dusk. It was a pleasant night with stars and even a sickle-moon. There was a scent of flowers, something he had never noticed before in Soledad. Maybe it wasn't flowers, maybe it was that flower-scent she wore.

At her adobe they halted and he held out a hand. She lay cool fingers on his palm and looked up without smiling. "I don't understand how something like this can happen so—suddenly."

His hand closed around her fingers. "A man waits a long time. I guess a woman does too."

"*Si*. A woman waits even longer. There are always men, so the wait is longer. When will you go up to Las Crucas?"

"The same day you will."

She smiled. "I think you move—a little fast."

"As slow as you like," he told her. "If I get too far ahead, just rein me up. I'll understand."

"Good night, Jim."

He walked, turned, saw her watching him, and waved. She waved back then entered the little house and he walked all the way back to Main Street without thinking of anything else, until a lanky man detached himself from shadows and said, "Mister Logan and your partner are waitin' at the jailhouse."

Even then it was hard for Doria to force his thoughts away from her, but he nodded and hiked across the road.

Someone had lighted the lamp and the stale-smelling small office seemed as drab as ever when Doria walked in. Spencer cocked an eye. "How's the old Mex?"

"Fine," Doria answered. "He was sleeping and he's got some kinsmen lookin' after him."

"What did he have to say?"

Doria went to a chair, eyed Marshal Logan, then turned toward his partner. "To tell you the truth, Paul, I didn't see him."

"Then how do you know he's all right?"

"I—was told he was all right." Doria felt annoyance. "What have you two been cooking up?"

"We're free," said Spencer. "He's not going to arrest us."

Doria faced the hard-eyed lawman. "Is that true?"

"Yeah. I guess so. I got Spencer's word and now I need your word. No more outlawing. No matter what nor where—no more outlawing. Your word on it."

"That's all? Then we're free?"

Logan inclined his head without speaking.

"You got it," stated Doria. "You got my word no more outlawing—no matter what."

Spencer smiled widely. "What did I tell you, Marshal?"

157

Logan kept gazing at Jim Doria. "You ever been up around Las Crucas?"

Spencer's smile faded. He stared perplexedly at Marshal Logan. Jim Doria felt uncomfortable. He had a forming suspicion that, somehow or other, Marshal Logan knew about Eulalia Montoya. He shook his head. "I never been up there. But I figure to go up there soon. Why?"

"Nothing," said Logan, and arose to yawn then to go as far as the door before speaking again. "You can have those horses you stole from Alvarado. He probably stole them but they got Mex brands so it's not likely anyone is going to jump out and claim them. Spencer—good luck getting that saloon. Doria—good luck up in Las Crucas . . . I envy you."

Logan walked out into the night and Spencer brought his perplexed glance back to Doria. "What in hell was he talking about—Las Crucas?"

"It's a town up north." Doria lamely said, and got busy rolling a smoke. "You want to ride along?"

"And stay in this damned territory?" exclaimed Paul Spencer. "Not on your darned life I don't want to ride along. Me, I'm heading back up north and I'm not going to quit riding until I've got a decent riding job in Montana—or maybe Wyoming. I'm going to save up some money and get that saloon . . . Las Crucas? What in hell do you want to go up there for? You never mentioned the place before."

"Oh," mused Doria, trickling smoke, "maybe I'll hire on up there. And get married."

Spencer forgot his injured ankle and dropped both feet to the floor—then cursed as pain shot up his leg. He eased the injured leg out and gently set it down again, very gently.

"Married! You get married?" He started to say something more, then checked himself. "Las Crucas—married? What the hell is this all about? That federal deputy knew something—I could tell by watching him. What's going on?"

Doria blew smoke and smiled through it. "Nothing is going on. Not yet anyway. I just want to go up around Las Crucas. It's no crime as far as I know."

Spencer got to his feet using that stick he had found to keep most of the weight off his wrenched ankle. In loud disgust he said, "My boot better still be lyin' out there. I'm going down to the liverybarn and burrow into a shock of hay."

Doria nodded and continued to sit and smoke and gaze at the far wall—and softly smile.

Center Point Publishing

600 Brooks Road • PO Box 1
Thorndike ME 04986-0001 USA

(207) 568-3717

US & Canada:
1 800 929-9108
www.centerpointlargeprint.com